A St. Louis L
My

By: National Bestselling Author
T'Ann Marie

KENEKU
1/24/18

T'Ann Marie

Chapter One

Gwahla sat in the interrogation room at the cold, steel, rectangular shaped table, as he nervously bounced his left leg up and down expeditiously, while biting his nails. He had been waiting forever on the detectives to come in to take his statement. He wished they would hurry the fuck up because he still had Zaria waiting for him in the car. A part of him couldn't believe what the hell he was about to do, but he had to do it. Where he was from, snitching was the quickest way to get you sent up to them pearly gates, but he felt it was the only way to keep he and Zaria safe.

He was shocked and caught off guard seeing Fragile out in the store. Not to mention, her being with one of the niggas he'd paid to knock off Marcus, while recording him with Zaria. She was right, the shit just made too much sense to be a coincidence. Plus, word around the streets was Fatz had it out for him, for sending niggas out to work on his blocks, and he knew that nigga always made good on his threats. Gwahla was sure those two were up to something, so he had to get them before they got him.

Sighing deeply, he ran his hands over his low, cut Caesar with deep waves. Just as he was about to get up and see what was taking them pigs so long, in walked two homicide detectives. One was a Mexican man, who appeared to be in his mid to late forties. He was sporting a white, long sleeved, collared dress shirt, and a burgundy tie. The khaki colored slacks he wore, were pulled all the way up over his beer belly and his black, leather belt matched his cheap, leather shoes. Not to mention his slick bald head and Steve Harvey mustache; he looked like a character that belonged in the cartoon, Family Guy.

"Good evening. I am detective Morales, and this is my partner detective Harrington." He referred to the smooth, caramel, skin brother to the left of him; who was dressed as sharp as a tack in his smoked grey, three-piece suit. His salt and peppered, curly box fade, and dark brown eyes sort of put you in the mind frame of the actor Denzel Washington when you looked at him. He too appeared to be in his mid to late forties but wore it well.

"How are you gentleman doing?" Gwalah stood up to shake both of their hands. The detectives sat in the two chairs across from him as he sat back in his seat.

"We're quite well. Even better since we have you here. We hear you may have a break in the case we've been on for a few months now." Detective Harrington spoke up. Gwalah swallowed hard as he looked the two detectives, square in their faces. At that moment her regretted even walking into the station and wanted to get his ass up to walk right back out, but he knew it was a little too late for that.

"Uhm, yeah. Yeah, I think I may be able to shed some light on that incident." He bobbed his head up and down in assurance.

"Okay, great." Detective Morales stated, scribbling something onto the notepad he had in front of him. Reaching into his suit jacket pocket, his partner pulled out a tape recorder. Just as he was about to turn it on, Gwahla stopped him.

"Ayo, my man, what's that for?" He asked looking at detective Harrington as if he was doing something out of the ordinary. He gave Gwalah a slight chuckle.

"I'm getting ready to record your statement, what does it look like?" the detective looked at him like he was dumb.

"I mean, you gotta do all of that?" he pointed from the tape recorder, to the notepad. "I thought I just come up in here, tell y'all what I know in confidence, y'all let me go, and go do y'all jobs and shit. I ain't tryna be on nobody's tape recorder or in nobody's

4

paperwork." He said honestly. The two detectives looked at one another then back to him.

"Listen, uuhm…"

"Gwalah." He was still debating on if he wanted to give them his real name or not.

"Gwalah?" he bobbed his head. Detective Morales looked as if he wanted to ask what kind of name that was but decided against it. He didn't want to scare him off before he could get out of him, everything he knew about their case. So, he took another route.

"Okay, Mr. Gwahla. Believe me when I tell you that everything you share in here today is and will remain in confident. The notes that we are gathering are strictly for our records and benefit, only. Everything you say tonight will remain amongst us three and us three it will stay." Detective Harrington assured him.

Gwahla slumped down in his chair, folding his arms across his chest as he sucked his teeth, in deep thought. It was something about detective Harrington that made him feel a bit at ease. He guessed it was because he was a brother. He just hoped he wasn't one of them uncle Tom ass niggas.

"Iight, first things first, ima need to be placed under some type of protective custody. Me, my girl, and our babies." He told them.

"Done!" Detective Morales agreed, eagerly. "We'll have you all, put away right after you give your statement. My word is good." He continued. Gwalah stared at both cops thoroughly, as he continued sucking his teeth.

"I want us to be placed as far away as possible and I want 24-hour surveillance." He demanded.

"We can do that also." Detective Harrington assured him. Looking back and forth between the two, Gwalah studied their faces. They seemed to look like men of their word, so he decided to proceed.

Reaching into his pocket, he pulled out a pack of Newport shorts and a blue, Bic lighter. After firing up a cigarette he took a long pull and blew out a thick cloud of smoke.

"Iight, I'm ready." He gave them the green light to record his statement.

As Gwalah finished off his cancer stick, he told the dicks everything they wanted to know. His snake ass had officially become a rat as well.

∞∞∞

Chubbz walked out the front door of the trap, closing it behind him. After locking up all three, deadbolts, and the bottom knob, he turned and headed for his ride. Aiming his keypad towards his 2018, candy red, Kia Stinger, he unlocked the doors before hopping in. After starting it up, he sat there for a little minute as he pulled his phone from the pocket of his jeans and powered it back on.

He had been in the bando for the past few hours doing a count, up so he had turned his phone off, avoiding any interruptions. Since Fatz had been preoccupied with his newfound main thang, Chubbz had to do the count alone, so he couldn't afford any fuck ups. When his phone came on, it started buzzing and dinging like crazy, alerting him of all the missed calls and messages. He had a few calls from Fatz, a couple cluckers, and several text messages from many of his random thots. Smiling from ear to ear, his eyes landed on the voicemail that had Teyanna's name above it. Clicking on it, he punched in his voicemail password, placed the phone to his ear and waited for it to play. As he listened closely to the message, his smile slowly began to fade.

"What the fuck?" he said aloud, pulling the phone away from his ear. He grimaced at it for a second before putting it back.

He could hear the loud sounds of crashing, tussling, and Teyanna screaming as if she were being attacked. Chubbz was high off, of a pack and several loud blunts, but he knew he wasn't crazy. Her screams were kind of muffled, but he could clearly make out the words, *help me!*

Hanging up from his voicemail, he quickly dialed her up. He began to panic a bit when it went straight to her voicemail. His mind quickly reverted, back to when he'd spoken to her last. They were in the middle of texting and she'd just suddenly stopped. Being that they'd been talking for a while he knew she had a man, so when she did shit like that, he knew the bitch ass nigga was somewhere around.

Chubbz began to wonder if he'd gotten ahold of her phone and saw their messages. Hoping to get some different results, he hit Teyanna's line once more, but got the voicemail again. He bit down onto his lip in frustration. All kinds of thoughts were going on inside of his head and he didn't know which one to follow. On many occasions Teyanna would express how much of a hoe ass nigga, her man was and how they always argued, but she never said shit about him being abusive. The last thing he wanted to do was run up in they shit, and it was just another one of their bull-shit arguments; shit would really get real then. On the other hand, he would feel like shit if she was somewhere hurt and he didn't go see about it.

Scrolling to his brother's name, he clicked on it and dialed him up, hoping Fragile could at least tell him something. That became one less option when his phone went straight to voicemail as well. He couldn't understand what the fuck was up with every-body being unreachable.

"Fuck it!" he signed deeply, throwing his phone into the cup holder. He knew his decision was risky, but he just had to make sure his boo was safe. He wouldn't be able to rest if he didn't.

Reaching underneath his seat, he pulled out a chrome, 9mm Beretta, handgun, with the blue grip. Pulling out the clip, he was pleased to see that it was fully loaded. Slamming the clip back in, he sat it on the passenger seat before throwing his car into gear and doing the dash all the way to Teyanna's spot.

In ten minutes flat Chubbz was pulling up to her apartment complex. Quickly throwing his car in park, he shut of the lights and engine. Checking his surroundings, he made sure there weren't any witnesses. Yea, it was close to 2 in the morning but where he was from, there was always somebody out lurking; no matter the time of day. After seeing the coast was clear, he grabbed his gun from the passenger seat and hopped out of his ride. As he made his way up the stairs to her front door, he cocked it, getting ready for whatever. When he made it to the door, he began banging on it with the butt of his gun. After not getting an answer, he put his ear up to the door. It was so quiet on the other side you could hear a pin drop.

Pulling out his phone, he proceeded to try and get Teyanna on the phone once more. This time the phone began ringing and he could hear it going off on the inside of her apartment, letting him know that she had to be in there. Getting the voicemail again Chubbz ended the call, quickly pocketed his phone and began banging once more; this time a little harder. His adrenaline immediately began pumping when he finally heard the rambunctious, voice of a man.

"Who the fuck is it!" he yelled; Chubbz could hear movement behind the door. He placed his hand over the peep hole and remained quiet.

"Whoever the fuck you are, you got five seconds to get yo hand from over the fuckin peep hole and show yo face, before I blow ya ass off!" the guy threatened.

Chubbz was far from pussy and his heart didn't pump no fucking kool-aid either, so he decided to call his bluff and left his hand where it was. Before he knew it, he heard the locks unlatching and the door quickly flew open. Chubbz didn't know what to expect so he had his gun aimed, finger on the trigger, ready to shoot. Only to be standing gun to face, with a light skinned, mad nigga with a bat and no pistol. He was tough as a muthafucka before he opened the door, but when he realized he was staring down the barrel of a gun, the grimace he bore on his face softened and his cheeks began turning a flushed red color. Chubbz could see the bitch in his eyes and just knew he wanted to shit himself, but surprisingly he kept his game face on.

"Who the fuck, are you and what the fuck you doin at my crib?" Quincy asked, chunking his chin up.

"All that shit don't even matter, homeboy." Chubbz said, gun still pointed in his face. "Where the fuck is Teyanna at?" he continued.

Quincy chuckled.

"You got some nerve running up over here, pointing a gun up in my face, asking about my bitch!" He put emphasis on the word my.

Chubbz sucked his teeth. He could read people really, well and he could tell that Quincy was one of those bitch ass possessive ass niggas. It was taking everything in him not to blow his fucking head off, but he couldn't commit a homicide until he knew that Teyanna was okay. Once he knew that, he had no problem Swiss cheesing the nigga then getting them the fuck out of dodge.

Taking a good look at Quincy, Chubbz noticed a bunch of fresh scratches all over his face and neck, that he hadn't even paid attention to when he first opened the door. It looked as if the nigga had gotten into a fight with a cat, and that bitch won. Chubbz mind began to replay the message left on his phone of Teyanna screaming and his armpits instantly began to get hot. He could feel the situation about to turn into a homicide before he left the scene, but he continued to play it cool.

"Aye bruh, on some real shit just go get Teyanna and let me see her. I don't want no problems, I'm just here to check on her." He told him.

Quincy continued to laugh hard as fuck.

"Aw, shit! You really came!" he stated looking crazy as shit.

That's when Chubbz looked into his eyes and noticed the nigga was high off, of something. His eyes were bloodshot red, and his pupils were bigger than the size of a quarter. Not to mention the smell of liquor reeking from his pores. Chubbz now understood where his extra courage was coming from. He just hoped the nigga had a life insurance policy because if Teyanna was hurt in anyway, he was about to meet his creator.

"Nigga, what the fuck is you talking about?" Chubbz grimaced, referring to his last statement.

"She called, and you came. That's sweet, being that you the reason she layin up in there fu..."

Before he could finish his statement, Chubbz snatched him by the neck and rushed him inside of the apartment. He swiftly kicked the door closed as he bashed him in the mouth repeatedly, with the butt of his gun at the same time. After about the third hit, Quincy's body went limp and Chubbz could hear him snoring. Letting him go he dropped to the living room floor, next to the whole front row of his teeth.

Leaving his bitch ass there to nap, Cubbz made his way to the back of the apartment to look for Teyanna. Her place wasn't that big, so he knew she couldn't have been too many places. Heading straight for the bedroom, he noticed she wasn't in the bed like he assumed she would be. It was dark as a bitch in the apartment, so he was relying on the little bit of light that was seeping through the windows from the streetlights, to help him see.

Making his way to the bathroom connected to her bedroom, he flipped on the lights, only to see she wasn't in there either. He began to panic because there was no telling what that bitch ass nigga Quincy had done to her. Sighing deeply, he exited the bathroom and went back into the bedroom. Focusing his attention towards the closet he proceeded to head to it but was tripped up by something in the middle of the floor. After catching himself before he could fall, he looked down and noticed it was Teyanna. She was curled into a fetal position as she laid in a pool of her own blood, naked and motionless. Even though he had turned on the light in the bathroom it was still pretty, hard to see, but it was obvious that she was messed up pretty, bad.

"What the fuck, Teyanna." Chubbz whispered to himself as he kneeled, down to check her pulse, praying she still had one; She did.

Stuffing his gun inside his waist, he snatched a sheet from off, of the bed and wrapped her up in it. After she was fully covered, he scooped her up in his arms bridal style, and headed for the door. When he made it into the living room, Quincy was still laid out in the middle of the floor snoring. Chubbz wanted so badly to put a bullet between his eyes, but he had to get Teyanna to the hospital to get some help. He would definitely handle his bitch ass later though.

∞∞∞

"You sleep, babe?" Fatz whispered to Fragile, as they laid in the center of his king-sized bed, in a spooning position. He had his hand wrapped around her waist, as he slowly rubbed on her belly.

Ever since their little run in with Gwahla and Zaria back at Wal-Mart, she had been acting strange. The whole ride home she didn't say a word, just simply stared out of window. Even when Fatz would try to spark up a conversation with her, she would shut him down with a one, word response and continue staring out of the window. When they finally did make it back to his house, she wasn't interested in doing anything but going to bed. He didn't know what was up, being that he hadn't done anything wrong so he couldn't understand the all, of a sudden silent treatment. He knew one thing though, he didn't like it, and he was ready to get to the bottom of it.

"No, I'm up." Fragile replied, back softly.

"What's wrong? You've been on hush mode since we left the store, what's that about?" he asked. "And don't give me that you fine shit, because I know when something's fucking with you." He continued.

Fragile remained silent for a couple more seconds. Sighing deeply, she turned over, repositioning herself in the bed so that she could face him. For a moment she just stared in his eyes, as he did the same. Fragile couldn't lie, she liked the fuck out of Fatz. Hell, it was almost feeling like love, but she was trying her hardest not to fall. It was still so much she had to learn about him, even though it felt as if they'd known each other a lifetime; shit was just that comfortable.

"Can I ask you something and you keep it all the way real with me?" Fragile finally spoke, still gazing into his beautiful, brown eyes.

"Don't I always keep it G?" he asked. "When have I ever lied to you?"

Fragile shrugged. He had a point. The whole time they'd been dealing with one another he was honest, no matter how much she didn't like his truths. So, she didn't even know why she bothered asking him to keep it real.

"Yea, you right. My bad for even coming at you like that." She gave a half smile.

"It's all good. I get it. But what's up?" he asked eager to know her question.

"How do you know Gwhala?" she finally asked.

"Shit, to be honest I really don't know him, know him like that. I mean, he a street nigga and I'm in the streets. We've had dealings here and there but nothing like that. I can't fuck with him like that; I'm starting to see he a fuck nigga, and I can't fuck with his kind." Fatz sucked his teeth.

"Oh, okay." Fragile simply replied. Something about the way she said it didn't sit well with Fatz. He had a strong feeling it was more to why she asked that question.

"What's up, why you ask that?" he questioned.

"Oh, no reason. Was just curious, that's all." She shrugged. Fatz looked at her as he tried to figure her out. Sucking his teeth, he scoffed.

"So, how you know him?" he returned the question. "Looked to me you two got some history. Is he really ya ex and you lied to me saying he was dead, and he was just dead to you?" He insinuated.

"What?! No! Hell no!" Fragile scoffed offended. "Nothing like that. Not even fucking close!" she continued.

"So, how you know him? You seemed pretty tight that he was with ole girl. Then when we leave you quiet the whole time; it all makes sense. I mean if y'all used to fuck around I don't give a fuck, Fragile. That nigga is the past, I ain't worried about him." Fatz kept assuming he knew the deal.

"No, Brian! I said no. Gwalah isn't even my type, I would never date him." She stated in her defense.

"I mean, shit. You said the same shit about me too, and here we are." Fatz replied, thinking that he was proving a point. Fragile scoffed, sitting up in the bed.

"What the fuck is that supposed to mean? What are you trying to say?" She looked at him with attitude; his ass was really pushing it.

"I ain't tryna say shit but what I said. You asked me how I know him, and I told you. Now that I'm asking you the same shit, it seems like it's hard for you to answer. So, it gives me reason to believe y'all have history." Fatz explained.

Fragile became quiet for a moment as she sat deep in thought. Sighing deeply, she fondled with her fingernails as she began speaking.

"We do have history. I know him very well, but it's not how your thinking." She finally confessed.

"Meaning?" Fatz asked waiting for her to elaborate.

"Do we really have to talk about this, Brian? Because I honestly don't feel like it right now." She sighed.

"Yea, we do. It's mighty funny that whenever the spotlight is on me and you got shit you wanna know, you got all the time in the world. But when I ask shit, you never wanna talk about it. Nah, Fragile. You started the conversation, we gon finish it. So, what's up? I'm listening." Fatz sat up, scooting his back up against his headboard.

Fragile cut her eyes at him in frustration. What he didn't understand was, she avoided talking about anything concerning her past because she hated reliving it, not because she was hiding anything. She hated that she still couldn't talk about Chief and his murder without getting emotional. The last thing she want to do, was make him feel that she was still stuck on her ex, even if that was the case. Then again, she couldn't keep running away from the conversation forever, she had to talk about it with him sooner or later.

"Gwalah was the best friend of my child's father, Marcus. We were all together the night he was murdered on his 25th birthday, at the club." Fragile recited just above a whisper; Fatz's heart damn near dropped to his feet. Swallowing hard, he adjusted his position in the bed.

"Y..You, talkin about the cat that got hit up in his whip, leaving St. Louis Nights? I think they called him, Chief, or some shit like that?" he fished for more information before overreacting.

"Yeah." Fragile sighed, smacking her lips softly. "The shit was all over the news. Crazy thing is, I was in the car with him that night." She stared off into space. "The shit replays in my head, over and over, and still til this day, I don't understand how I didn't get hit. There were so many bullets!" Just like that, her tears began to flow.

Fatz sat there at a lost, for words as he watched Fragile cry her eyes out, as if the shit had just happened. As much as he hated to admit it, his heart ached for her. Not once, out of all the niggas he and his brother had murdered, did he ever feel a pinch of remorse, but seeing the way Fragile was breaking down, made him feel like shit behind Chief. How? Was all that kept running through his mind. How did he end up falling for the baby mother of a man he'd put out of his misery? The shit literally made him sick to his stomach.

The fucked, up part was, besides being rivals in the dope game, Fatz had never had a problem with Chief. Fatz would stay in his lane and Chief would stay in his; the shit was just business. He and his brother had been paid to do a job and they got it done. No different from any other hit they were hired to do. The shit wasn't personal. He just hated that it was coming back to bite his ass in the worst way possible.

"He died in my arms." Fragile sniffled, calming herself down. "After he died, I never heard another word from that punk ass nigga Gwahla. When we were at the police station the night of the murder, he acted as if he was so concerned about me. Told me that he had me and I would never have to worry about anything because I was his brother's girl and he loved me like a sister." She scoffed, shaking her head in disappointment. Fatz stayed silent as he listened to her vent.

"Something told me that all the shit he was saying was a damn lie, but I believed him. Just like I believed Cheif's lying as when he sold me all of those dreams my dumb ass bought. You know that sorry muthafucka didn't even inform me of the funeral arrangements?" she turned to look at Fatz. "Teyanna got the information from his mother's Facebook page. Ain't that a bitch?"

she asked as if she was waiting on a reply.

"Damn." Fatz uttered, shaking his head.

"Then I go to pay my respects to the nigga I'd been in love with for a whole fucking year, only to find out he has a whole nother family on my dumb ass." Just thinking about the shit made Fragile pissed all over again.

"Wait, what?" Fatz questioned making sure he'd heard her right.

"Yeah, you heard me. The bitch we saw in the store with Gwahla tonight is supposed to be Marcus's fiance', that's why I was acting the way I was. When you were busy looking at clothes for baby girl, I spotted them across the aisle. The nigga was kissing her belly and they were all boo'd up and shit. If she's supposed to be his dead homie's girl, what the fuck is he doing kissing all over her belly and shit? Friends don't do that shit to their friend's women. I would never let him kiss on my fucking belly, that's crossing the line. Don't you think?"

"Fuck yea, that's wild." Fatz played with his beard as he stared off into space taking everything in. Fragile had been through so much before they'd met, and it was making him sick to his stomach to know that he'd played a part in the reason her heart was hurting.

"You just don't understand how tired I am of being hurt and lied to. I just want to move on with my life and be happy." Fragile broke down crying, again.

Fatz scooted closer towards her, pulling her in for a hug. Fragile cried in his chest as he did his best to soothe and comfort her. Each whimper she let out made his heart break. In just a few months he had fallen in love with her, and now he had to deal with maybe losing forever after confessing his truth, because he was damn sure coming clean about what he'd done. There was no way he could be with Fragile and look her and baby girl in their faces every day, knowing that he'd taken the closest person to them, away from them. His conscience just wouldn't let him. He may have been cold, but he wasn't heartless. Especially when it came to Fragile.

"Babe." Fatz called just above a whisper, as a lonely tear managed to escape from his eyes. "I have to tell you something and it's serious." He continued.

Fragile lifted her head from his chest, wiping the tears from her face. Looking up at Fatz, she could see so many different emotions in his facial expression. She could tell that whatever he was about to say to her wasn't good and she wasn't ready for it. She had been through enough; she couldn't take any more bad news.

"Brian, if it's bad, please don't tell me. I am tired of bad news." She sniffled, drying the tears from her eyes.

"Before I met you, I thought I would never love or be happy again, but you proved me wrong. I know it sounds bad, but up until tonight, it had been weeks since I'd even thought about anything pertaining to Marcus and this situation. You've kept my mind away from all of that. I thank God every day because I know he sent you. I prayed for healing and peace, then along came you. I just want to enjoy my peace and continue to live in it. Please don't make me go back." Fragile spoke softly.

Fatz gazed deep into her eyes and saw the hurt. As bad as he wanted her to know the truth, he knew he couldn't cause her any more pain. Especially not after the way she'd poured her heart out. Leaning in their lips met, as they shared a strong, passionate kiss. There was no denying the chemistry between them was crazy, it was as if they were made for one another. Fatz turned her on in so many ways, that no one would ever believe that she wasn't attracted to him in the beginning. In her eyes everything about him was sexy. She loved all of him; from his beautiful light brown eyes, to his pudgy, tatted up gut. He was all hers.

Taking in the scent of his Dior Sauvage, cologne as they tongue danced, Fragile could feel her kitty quiver. It had been months since she'd been touched sexually and the way Fatz was

17

caressing her thigh, was causing a puddle to form in her panties. Pushing him back onto the bed, Fragile saddled herself up on top of him, grinding her pussy against his dick. She could feel him bricking up quickly, confirming that her suspicion about fat boys were wrong. All of them didn't have baby dicks; well, at least Fatz didn't. He was every bit of 9 inches. Her hormones were raging and all she wanted to do was feel him inside of her. She had so much pinned up frustration, it was time to release.

Reaching down between her legs, she proceeded to unfastening his belt and jeans. After unzipping them, she freed his member and began softly jacking it. Fatz let out a soft grunt as he bit down onto his bottom lip. The feel of his warm, pre-cum, oozing in the palm of her hand excited her even more. Putting her palm up to her face, she licked it clean, tasting all of him. It was a bit salty, yet sweet, nevertheless tasty. Pulling her black, laced panties to the side, she grabbed his rock, hard dick and commenced to rubbing the tip against her slippery, wet, pearl.

"You sure you ready for this?" Fatz asked, interrupting her groove.

He knew she was vulnerable at that moment and he didn't want her making any sudden decisions based off, of emotions. On many occasions, Fragile had expressed how she didn't want to have sex with him while pregnant with another man's baby, so he wanted to be sure that she was aware of what she was about to do.

"Yes, yes, I'm sure!" Fragile moaned, glaring at him with lustful eyes. Biting down onto her bottom, lip, her whole facial expression screamed *fuck me,* as she continued to grind on him in a circular motion.

Aggressively, grabbing him by the collar of his t-shirt, Fragile pulled Fatz in for another sloppy kiss. Gripping her pillow soft, ass, he caressed it with both hands, as she let out soft, purrs. She wanted him so bad, it felt as if her pussy had a heartbeat of its own. Not being able to hold out any longer, Fragile pushed Fatz back onto his back.

"Take this shit off!" he demanded, pulling the sleeper that graced her body, over her head. When it was off, he admired her beautiful, full, breast. Even with her being nine months pregnant, they sat up nice; nipples sticking straight forward. Fatz licked his lips at the sight before him. Fragile was beautiful as fuck.

Grabbing his rock hard, dick, she positioned it at the opening of her pussy. Sliding down on him slow, they both gasped in ecstasy as the enjoyed the feeling of one another. Bouncing up and down with caution, she took it easy until her kitty warmed up to the size of him. Once the slight pain turned into pleasure, Fragile picked up the pace, resting both hands on his smooth, tattooed chest, gazing down into his beautiful eyes.

"Oh my gosh, you feel so good." Fragile whispered through moans. She could feel herself on the verge of bussing a nut, just that fast.

"Nah, that pussy feel good on this dick." Fatz grunted, giving her ass a light smack. "Cum for daddy, baby." He demanded.

Reaching up, he began fondling her hard, Hershey kiss, shaped nipples. Throwing her head back in ecstasy, she rode his dick like a brand, new Harley Davidson, rolling her hips in a circular motion. Fragile was so wet she could hear the sounds of her pussy gushing beneath her. That and the way Fatz was hitting her g-spot, had her right at the tip of her peak.

"Oh my God, baby! I'm about to cum!" Fragile screamed, digging her hot pink, stiletto shaped nails, into his chest.

"That's what the fuck I'm talkin about, give that shit to daddy!" Fatz grunted, throwing dick right back at her.

"Oh yes, oh yes, I'm right there, baby, it's coming!"

"Come on with it!"

"Oh shit, oh shit! Oooooh shiiiiiit!" Fragile climaxed.

Next thing they knew, they heard a weird noise and water began gushing from out of her, all onto Fatz pelvis and belly. Feeling a sharp pain in her side and abdomen, Fragile doubled over, yelping out in pain.

"What the fuck?! What the fuck?!" Fatz panicked, still inside of her. "Bae, you iight? Did I hurt you?" he questioned, frantic.

"No, no, I'm good. But I think my water just broke, Brian." She replied calmly.

"Y..you think what?!" Fatz was nervous as hell. He couldn't understand how she was so calm, and her water had broken.

"We gotta get to the hospital, Brian. It's time!" She stated, climbing from off top of him.

Fragile was so embarrassed. She couldn't believe she had gone into labor while bussing a nut!

Chapter Two

"Look Glammy! Cheeeeese!" MJ boasted, pointing his little finger at his freshly brushed teeth.

"Yeah, I see! That's Glammy's big boy! Brushing your teeth all by yourself!" Ms. Jefferson smiled, as she reached out and softly pinched her grandson's cheeks. "Give Glammy high five!" She held her hand up and MJ slapped it.

"Now rinse off your toothbrush and put it back into the toothbrush holder like Glammy taught you."

Turning the water back on, he did as he was asked. Ms. Jefferson stood back as she watched MJ stand on top of the toilet, leaning over the sink. After rinsing his toothbrush off, he lightly tapped it on the edge of the sink before placing it back in the toothbrush holder. Ms. Jefferson slightly chucked. She made a mental note to be very careful of the things she did in front of MJ, because he was literally mocking her every move. Turning the water off, he climbed down from the toilet and wiped his damp hands onto his pajama pants.

"All done!" He looked up giving her a smile, looking just like his father.

Ms. Jefferson admired her grandson as she tried to hold back the tears. Everything about him reminded her of Marcus, causing her to miss him more and more as the days and months went by. She wished so bad that she could turn back the hands of time and bring him back. Just about every day she thought about what she could have done to save her son from the bullets that took him away from them; even though she wasn't anywhere around that night. She was his mother. She was supposed to protect him from all hurt, harm and danger. Well, at least that's what she kept telling herself.

"Glammy, can we go make pamcakes now?" MJ questioned, breaking her from her thoughts. Snickering at his comment, she picked him up and tossed him on her hip.

"It's PANcakes, baby. And yes, we can go make some now." Ms. Jefferson smiled exiting the bathroom, heading toward the kitchen.

"Yaaaay! I love pamcakes!"

"You doooo?!" Ms. Jefferson played along as if the news was new to her.

"Uh huh! At my house, uncle T makes me banana pamcakes!" he told her excitedly.

"Uncle T?" Ms. Jefferson's face scrunched up in confusion. "What's uncle T doing at your house that early to be able to make you banana pancakes?" She asked curious as hell.

Yea, she knew Terrance and Zaria had been keeping in touch since her son died, checking on her and MJ every now and then, but she didn't think they were that close for him to be cooking all up in her kitchen, making breakfast.

"W..When he sleep in the bed with me and mommy, he wake up and makes me pamcakes. Then I go to school." He told her, not knowing that he was telling a little too much.

"Sleep in the bed with you and mommy?!" Ms. Jefferson's heart dropped as she repeated her grandson's words. "Does he take you to school too?" She asked, needing to know a little more.

She knew that it was wrong to fish for information from a kid, but he had already told a little, so she wanted to know it all. What the hell was Terrence doing sleeping in the bed with Zaria and her grandson? What type of shit did they have going on? Something wasn't right and she was going to get to the bottom of it, once she got all, of the information she needed from MJ. She had

22

already been feeling some type of way about those two, due to them being so concerned about her son's assets. So, the things MJ were sharing with her, was only adding fuel to her already burning curiosity.

"Yes. He takes me to school in his black spaceship!" MJ nodded his head as his grandmother sat him in one of the chairs at the kitchen table.

Ms. Jefferson stood at the table, staring off into space, as she put it all together. She knew for a fact that MJ wasn't telling any fibs. About six months before Marcus had passed, he and Terrence had gone out and bought matching Lamborghini Urus, trucks; they called them their spaceships. Taking a seat at the table, she took a deep breath. She could feel her anxiety kicking in, so she practiced calming herself, before she went into a full panic attack. Ever since Marcus's passing, she'd been experiencing them rather frequently.

Ms. Jefferson was trying her best not to overreact, but shit wasn't adding up. She prayed to God that the things that she, were thinking weren't as they seemed. She loved Terrence as if he was her own son, and Zaria as she were her own daughter. She'd fed them, clothed them, treated them like they were hers. Not to mention all, of the shit her son had done. It was because of him they lived so lavishly. There was no way they could ever betray them in such manner.

"What about my pamcakes, Glammy?" MJ asked, breaking his grandmother from her thoughts.

"Glammy's sorry, boo. I'm getting on that right now." She got up from the table. Heading over to the pantry, she grabbed the Aunt Jemima pancake mix. "You want some apple juice while you wait?" She asked.

"Yes ma'am." His little voice replied. After pouring her grand baby a small cup of apple juice, Ms. Jefferson then proceeded to make his pancakes; all while thinking of the shit MJ had just laid on her brain.

Ding, dong!

Just as Ms. Jefferson was cutting up MJ's pancakes, the sound of the doorbell echoed through her home.

"Uh, oooh! Somebody's at the dooooor!" MJ sang as he stood up in his chair.

Quickly pouring the syrup on top of his hot cakes, she grabbed a Spider-Man, fork from the silverware drawer and placed the matching plate in front of him.

"Sit down and eat your food. Glammy's going to see who's at the door, okay."

"Okaaay." MJ whined as he sat down and did as he was asked.

Taking off towards the front of the house, Ms. Jefferson walked as fast as she could. Just as she was almost at the door, whomever was on the other side, began knocking.

"Coming!" she sang approaching the door. Without even looking out of the shades, she opened, up; coming face to face with two men dressed in black suits.

"Hello." She looked back and forth between the two. "Can I help you?" She asked curiously.

"Good morning. I am detective Morales, and this is my partner detective Harrington. We're are looking for Mrs. Minetta Jefferson." The Mexican one spoke up.

"That's Ms." She corrected him. "And I am she, what can I do for you?" She asked with attitude.

Ms. Jefferson couldn't hide the fact that she was pissed. Marcus had been gone three months and those muthafuckas were just now showing up at her doorstep. Not to mention the numerous calls to the station she'd made regarding the status of his case; just for them to tell her that they were still working and would contact her when they'd gotten more leads.

"Well we have a couple of leads on your son's case, and we were wondering if you had a moment to answer a couple of questions?" Detective Morales asked. Ms. Jefferson stood there for a quick second as she stared them up and down before finally making her decision.

"Sure. I guess that's fine." She stepped to the side, inviting them in.

"What a lovely home you have." The other detective, Harrington, complimented as he admired the décor of her home.

"Thanks. You guys can have a seat on the sofa." She led them into the family room. "Can I get you gentlemen anything? Juice, coffee?" She really wasn't in a friendly mood, but she knew it was the courteous thing to do.

"No thanks." Detective Morales replied as detective Harrington shook his head no. "If you will, we'll just like to get down to business. The sooner we get all of the answers and leads we need, the sooner we'll be able to solve your son's case." Detective Morales continued.

"O..okay." Ms. Jefferson swallowed hard as she clenched her chest. Taking a seat on the sofa across from detective Morales, next to detective Harrington, she shifted in her seat, preparing herself for whatever they were about to say. "So..?" She stated, letting them knows she was all ears.

"So, we had someone come forth with some information. Actually, someone who claims to know you and your son very well." Morales stated causing Ms. Jefferson's face to scrunch up in confusion.

"And who might that be?" She asked immediately.

Reaching into his black, leather briefcase, detective Morales pulled out a manila folder filled with papers. Opening it up he skimmed through his notes.

"Would you happen to know a, Terrance Cook?" he then asked.

"Yea, that's my son." She replied with a puzzled look; her

25

stomach, turning flips.

"Your son?" Harrington chimed in.

"Well, not my blood son, but he's like my son. He lost his biological mother when he was just ten years old, so I took him in. He and my son had been close long before then though." Ms. Jefferson clarified.

"Oh, I see." Detective Harrington nodded his head. Ms. Jefferson gave a look of confusion.

"Okay, I'm a little lost. What is going on and what does this have to do with Terrance?" She asked looking back and forth between the two detectives, waiting on either of their responses.

"Well, he was the person who came forward." Detective Morales confirmed.

"Wait, what?! How is that so? Terrence told me out of his own mouth that he wasn't there, that he didn't see anything. So, now you're telling me that he's changed his story?" She asked trying to get an understanding of it all.

"That's exactly what we're saying." Harrington stated. Mrs. Jefferson shook her head defiantly.

"Uh, un. No, something ain't right." She stated, looking at no one in particular. "He just wouldn't up and change his statement like that." She continued.

"Well, on top of changing his statement, he's asked to be placed in protective custody. So, there could be a chance that the suspect could be out to get him as well." Detective Morales informed her.

Ms. Jefferson sighed stressfully as she ran her hand over her low cut, natural, blonde, hair. She couldn't believe what her ears were receiving. The things MJ had said, plus the detective's words had her mind on overload, and it was barely even noon. She was trying to put it all together, but only ended up giving herself more of a headache.

"Glammyyy!" MJ called right before she heard his little feet running into her direction. "I'm done with my pamcakes. Can I have some more, pleeeease?" He begged, once making it into the entry of the family room; his little lips and cheeks just glistening, from syrup stains. Ms. Jefferson slightly chuckled.

"Excuse me." She told the detectives before turning her attention back to her grandson. "I keep telling you it's PANcakes, baby. Not pamcakes." She snickered. "And yes, you can have some more. Just go back in the kitchen and give Glammy a few more minutes with these nice gentlemen, kay. I'll be right there." She continued.

"Kay!" MJ smiled brightly. "Hi!" He then chirped, waving his little hand at the detectives. They both chuckled, returning the smiles.

"Hey little guy!" Harrington replied.

Detective Morales simply waved reciting, "Such a handsome little fella." as MJ ran back to the kitchen.

"Thank you!" Ms. Jefferson smiled. "He's a handful and as smart as a whip." She continued.

"I bet. How old is he?" Detective Morales asked.

"Three, going on thirty-three!" She joked and they all shared a chuckle.

"You can't help but love when they're that age though. I miss my kids being that small." Harrington chimed in.

"True." Ms. Jefferson agreed. "I don't mean to be rude, but can we please get back to the case." She got back to the task at hand.

"Oh, most definitely." Morales assured her.

"Now, why did Terrance ask to be protected? What kind of mess is he caught up in, detective?" She asked curiously.

"Ms. Jefferson, we may never know the truth to that question, but we do have the names of the potential suspects. Some that I was hoping you can identify and maybe put a face to them."

Ms. Jefferson swallowed hard, praying that they didn't give her a name of someone she'd might've known. Nodding her head in an up and down motion, she silently agreed to his statement. She was willing to help them out in any way possible, if it meant getting justice for her baby boy.

"Okay, great." Detective Morales stated as he pulled out the notes, he'd jotted down from Gwahla's statement.

Ms. Jefferson looked on in anticipation as her palms began to get sweaty. Rubbing them against the knees of her khaki colored, house pants, she tried sneaking peeks of the paperwork, but couldn't make out the font; it was too small. She cursed herself in her head for not having her second pair of eyes near. She wanted so badly to call out to MJ to bring her, her eyeglasses, but didn't want to alarm the detectives of her nosiness. There were a host of questions swarming around her brain that she wanted to ask, but she knew they couldn't and wouldn't give her the answers. So, she patiently sat, waiting for him to finish fumbling through his notes, to give her the small piece of info that he could reveal.

"So, Ms. Jefferson," Detective Morales looked up from his notes. "Would the name Brian Myers ring a bell? Possibly known as Fatz to the streets."

"Uhm, n...no." She stated looking him in the eyes. "I've never heard that name before a day in my life. I..is that who murdered my Marcus?" She asked desperately; eyes pleading with sorrow. Detective Morales formed his mouth to say yes but was quickly interrupted by his partner.

"Possibly." Harrington stated truthfully as he gave Morales a stern stare. "As of right now we're simply going off, of word of mouth as we investigate and try to put all of the pieces to the puzzle together. That is why we are here with you, to get as much valuable information as possible." He went on.

"Okay that's understandable, detective but as I said, I've

never heard that name in my life. Not from my son, not from anyone." She replied honestly.

"What about the name, Fragile Banks?" He then asked causing her heart to skip a beat.

"What did you say? C...come again." She stuttered. Both Morales and Harrington could sense the slight shift in her demeanor.

"Fragile Banks?"

Ms. Jefferson sat in silence as she starred off into space. She began to think of the first day her son had brought Fragile to her home, to the day she showed up at his funeral, to the day her son's lawyer read off his will; leaving just about everything he'd owned to her. Ms. Jefferson didn't know much about Ms. Fragile, but she knew for a fact that she was more than just an assistant. She was just trying to figure out what her name was doing exiting the homicide detective's mouth.

"Ms. Jefferson?" Morales snapped her from her thoughts.

"Yes." She simply stated slowly nodding her head up and down, still staring into space. Everything that she was taking in was making he numb all over again; more, numb than the day she'd found out her son had passed.

"Yes? Yes what?" Morales asked not knowing if she was answering the question or him calling her name.

"Yes.. yes, I know of her." Ms. Jefferson finally managed to admit as she focused her attention back toward them.

"May we ask how?" Morales questioned.

"Well about a year ago, my son brought her to my house. He told me that she was just an assistant of his, but I knew otherwise." She smacked her lips, lightly. "That boy was sleeping with that girl." She continued. Detective Harrington looked at his partner then back at Ms. Jefferson.

"What made you so sure?" he then asked.

"Because I just knew." She slightly shrugged. "A mother knows everything. It was way more than just business between those two. That child was in love with Marcus, I could see it all in her eyes." She finished.

"But he didn't tell you that verbatim, did he?"

"No. But, I know my child, detective." Ms. Jefferson stressed.

"Well if you knew him so well, why wouldn't he tell you about his relationship involving miss Banks?" detective Morales threw out another question.

Ms. Jefferson shifted in her seat as she gave him a blank stare. Morales was really starting to make her a bit uncomfortable. He was interrogating her as if she were the damn suspect, instead of the victim's grieving, mother. If it wasn't for detective Harrington's presence, she would have been ended their little meeting. Sighing deeply, Ms. Jefferson gained her composure as she continued to answer their questions.

"My son was engaged to his child's mother, Zaria. Their relationship was rocky, and they were having a number of problems. My son wanted to call it quits, but she wasn't having it. He would tell me that she would threaten to keep MJ away if he'd ever left. So, until he and his lawyer had all their ducks in a row, as far as custody, he decided to stay with her. We would speak on occasions about the things he'd had going on, but for the most part, my son was a private person. He really didn't like sharing his personal life with me because he didn't like the advice I would give. I mean, I'm a fair person, no matter what the situation is, and I tried raising my children to be the same. You do unto folks what you want done unto you; I stressed that all the time." She bobbed her head.

"I see." Detective Morales nodded. "So, you really don't know if your son and Miss Banks had more of a business relationship, you just assume, right?" He continued.

"Let me ask you something detective," Ms. Jefferson looked at him seriously, her dark brown eyes piercing through his. Morales bobbed his head assuring her that he was listening. "The day the good Lord decides your work is done, and it's time for you to leave this earth, are you going to leave everything you've worked so hard for, with your damn assistant?" she asked with venom on the tip of her tongue. Detective Morales chuckled a bit as he looked at his partner, right back to Ms. Jefferson.

"No, that would be ridiculous. Why would I do something crazy like that?" He asked not knowing where she was getting at.

"Then why would my son?!" She spat coldly. If looks could kill, Detective Morales would have been one dead enchilada.

"Wait, so you're saying that your son left all of his assets to miss Banks?" detective Harrington chimed in, curiously.

"Yes. According to his lawyer, he modified his Will just a few months prior to his death. Why he did it, I don't know." She confirmed. "But I know my son; and I know he had to be deeply in love with this girl in order to have left her everything he'd owned."

"Or threatened." Detective Harrington mumbled underneath his breath, as he toyed with his neatly trimmed salt and pepper goatee, in deep thought.

"What did you say?" Ms. Jefferson snapped her neck in his direction.

"Oh, nothing." He shook his head. "Ms. Jefferson, I want you to think back to the last few weeks before your son's death, how was he acting? Did he seem afraid? More alert than usual; as if someone were out to get him?" Harrington questioned. Ms. Jefferson shook her head expeditiously.

"No, no, my son was good. He was his regular normal happy self. I mean he was always cautious about the way he moved, but that was just him." She explained getting a slight bit irritated with all, of the ridiculous questions.

She so deeply wished that they'd get to the point already, so that she could escort them out of her home and get back to MJ. Yeah, she knew the life her son lived, but he was still her son; yet they were making it seem like he was the suspect and not the victim. So far, they hadn't provided her with any useful information, and she was over the interrogation.

"Not to seem rude but can you gentlemen please get to the point and share with me what's really going on? I really need to be getting back to my grandson." Ms. Jefferson stated calmly. She was growing tired of the beating around the bush.

"Well, Ms. Jefferson, we're just trying to do our jobs. Before we make any kind of assumptions, we have to gather all of the facts. We have some ideas of what may have happened to your son, but we can't say until we're certain."

"And what might those ideas be?" She questioned.

Detective Morales cleared his throat before gathering his notes, placing them back into his briefcase.

"Unfortunately, Ms. Jefferson, that information we won't be able to share with you at the moment." He stated standing to his feet. "We will be in touch with updates regarding the investigation, though." He gave a faint smile, reaching his stubby hand out for a handshake. Ms. Jefferson scoffed as she rose from the couch, slowly. Extending her arm, she gave his hand a weak shake, all while giving him an eerie once over.

"Well, okay then." She looked over at detective Harrington, as Morales was making his way to the door to let himself out. Harrington gave a slight smile as he took her hand into his. He could sense her uneasiness and it didn't sit well with him; his partner really could be a dick at times.

"Hang in there, ma'am. I promise we will do everything in our power to get justice for you and your family." Harrington stated, sincerely gazing into her eyes.

"Thank you." Ms. Jefferson replied just above a whisper.

"Take care and enjoy the rest of your day." He turned and walked out of the already opened door.

Sighing deeply, Ms. Jefferson closed the door behind him, locking it. Turning around, she pressed her back up against the door; a lonely tear escaped her right eye. So many thoughts consumed her mind it was unhealthy. What really happened to her son? Was all she could think. Breaking her from her thoughts, she began hearing MJ calling her from the kitchen.

"Glaaammyy! I'm ready for my pamcakes agaaaain!" his little voice sang. Quickly pulling herself together, she took a deep breath and wiped her face.

"Okaaay! I'm on my waaaay!" She then replied making her way back towards the kitchen.

Morales and Harrington had to be some damn fools if they thought she was going to sit back and wait for them to solve her son's case. With the little information she had, she was going to conduct her own little investigation.

Chapter Three

Chubbz sat on the edge of his seat at Tyanna's bedside, as he watched her sleep peacefully. He was hotter than fish grease looking at all, of the bruises, scratches and pain that Quincy's punk ass had left her to suffer with. Two black eyes, a busted lip, and a fractured jaw, was just the damage done to her face. He'd also left her with two broken fingers, and a few broken ribs. Not to mention the many knots, scratches, and rug burns, that rested sporadically over her skin. His punk ass had really put a beaten on Tyanna and Chubbz felt like he needed to put something on him. He wanted so badly to go back over to her place and smoke his bitch ass, and in due time he would. Until then, he just wanted to be the first face Teyanna saw whenever she woke up. Due to the heavy amount of pain meds the doctors had her on, she had been knocked out cold. Her vitals, EKG, and bloodwork all checked out well, so they decided to just let her rest.

Pulling up his call log, Chubbz clicked on the last person he'd been calling all night long, Fatz. He had been blowing the nigga's phone up since the minute he'd brought Teyanna into the emergency room, but the muthafucka kept going to voicemail. He knew for a fact that he was somewhere laid up with Fragile, and he needed Fatz to pass the news to her about her friend. But, just like the previous countless calls, it went to voicemail. Sighing deeply he clicked the end button, before burying his face into the palm of his hands. He couldn't even leave the nigga a damn message because his mailbox was full. His brother was the only nigga he knew who didn't check his messages, what kind of shit was that?

As he rested his face in his hands, Chubbz could feel himself beginning to doze off. It was going on twenty-six, hours since he'd had any sleep and the shit was starting to catch up to him, but he refused to leave Teyanna alone. Though it had only been a few months since they'd met, he'd developed feelings for Teyanna and he cared about her well, being; it was imperative that she knew he'd been there with her every step of the way.

As Chubbz rested his eyes he heard movement coming from the bed, causing him to look up. Focusing his attention on Teyanna, he noticed that she was awake. Her eyes were wide open and he could tell that she was trying to figure out where she was. Grabbing ahold to the side of the bed she scooted herself up, wincing in pain.

"Aye, chill. You can't be doing all that right now." Chubbz stated, jumping to her aid.

"What?" She looked at him confused. "What am I doing here?" She then asked.

"Uh, getting treated." He smacked his lips sarcastically, taking a seat back in his chair.

Sighing deeply, Teyanna laid back in the bed. Staring up at the ceiling she remained silent, as the last thing she could remember replayed over in her head. She remembered arguing with Quincy, but she couldn't remember why. She even remembered him attacking her and calling Chubbz, she just didn't remember him coming. Nevertheless, she thanked God that he did. She was so embarrassed that he'd witnessed her at such a vulnerable time, but she knew he wouldn't judge. That's what she loved about him.

"So, when were you going to tell me that that nigga was beating yo ass, Teyanna?" He broke the silence.

"I didn't know I was supposed to tell you that." She replied, still looking at the ceiling.

"Fuck you mean?! You open your mouth and say everything else, how the hell you forget to mention that?" He seethed.

"I mean, what the hell was I supposed to say, Chubbz? Hey, my name Teyanna nice to meet you. Oh, by the way, my boyfriend beats my ass, will you please save me?" She mocked, rolling her eyes to the top of her head.

"Come on man; don't be no ass. You could have found a way to tell me this shit, Teyanna. You find a way to tell me everything else about the weak ass nigga." He sucked his teeth; he was hot. It was so much more he wanted to say, but he didn't want to upset her; she was already going through enough. The last thing he wanted to do was add to her problems, so he remained quiet.

"You not goin back to that damn apartment." Chubbz finally stated, after breaking about five minutes, worth of silence.

"What? What you mean? Where the hell, am I supposed to stay?" Teyanna quizzed, confusedly.

"You can stay with me for the time being, but as long as that nigga is still walking around this bitch breathing, you're not going back home." He told her. Teyeanna sighed deeply as she slumped down in the hospital bed, folding her arms across her chest.

"Yea, okay." She stated dryly, smacking her lips.

Chubbz could tell that Teyanna had a little attitude, but he really didn't give a damn. Little did she know, she wouldn't have to stay with him long, just until he'd dead the nigga. After that, she could go back to her normal life. He didn't want to just flat out tell her that he was going to murder her little punk ass boyfriend; he didn't know if she could be trusted with that type of information just yet. Nevertheless, he was going to make sure she would never have to worry about Quincy hurting her again.

"Does Fragile know about this shit?" Chubbz asked.

"No, and you bet not tell her." Teyanna spat.

"Bullshit!"

"The hell is that supposed to mean? I said don't tell her!"

"Really, Teyanna? You laid up in the fuckin hospital bed, because some punk ass nigga dun beat you half to death, and you're telling me not to tell your best friend? What the fuck type of time you on, bruh? You gon take yo ass right back to that nigga, ain't you?"

Teyanna didn't say a word. She just stared off into space, as tears began to weld up in her eyes. Her mind was so lost, she didn't know what to do. She was mentally and physically tired of Quincy and wanted out so badly, but her heart wasn't ready to let him go. No matter how much he'd beaten her, he was all she knew. She was content where she was and starting over was something she just wasn't ready for. Her biggest fear was falling for another man, and he ended up just like Quincy.

"So, what did you call me for, Teyanna. I can tell by the way you're acting you're not over this dude." Chubbz gritted his teeth together in frustration. He couldn't deny, he liked Teyanna a lot, but if she wanted to be with a nigga who treated her like a fucking human punching bag, by all means he was going to let her have that.

"Byron, you don't understand." Tears began to fall from Teyanna's eyes.

"Nah," Chubbz sucked his teeth. "I don't. What is there to understand about a nigga that's beating the fuck out of you, Teyanna? You need to shake that punk ass nigga. You that ins.."

"I DON'T HAVE NOBODY!" Teyanna screamed, interrupting him in mid rant. "Quincy is all I have. Don't nobody care about me. I grew up taking care of myself, while I watched my mother let a nigga use and abuse her! When I met Quincy, I was down bad, and he helped me. He showed me the love that nobody has ever shown me." She cried uncontrollably. "Not even my own fuckin mother!"

Chubbz stood there speechless as fuck; suddenly he felt like shit. He was always told to never judge a book by its cover, and that was exactly what he'd done to Teyanna. He judged her situation before he even knew her background, and he was regretting it. Coming from a rough past himself, he knew what it was like to want to be loved. Hell, he was still searching for it.

Sighing deeply, Chubbz stepped closer to Teyanna's bedside, taking a seat on the edge of the bed. Grabbing her hand, he placed it in his, and began caressing it, while wiping away her tears with his other.

"Look man, I'm sorry. I'm an asshole for what I just said, and I hope you can forgive me. But you don't have to take that shit no more, Teyanna. When you get up out of here, just come home with me. I can love you way better than that weak ass nigga ever can, believe that. Just give me the chance to show you. A real nigga will never put his hands on you; I don't give a fuck how mad he gets. You're a queen and supposed to be treated as such." He stressed.

Teyanna and Chubbz had only been talking a few months yet had become very close. They talked on the phone a lot, but never really got too personal. They knew the basics about one another like government names, numbers of siblings, names of high schools, and shit like that, but that was about it. He was basically her breath of fresh air when Quincy wasn't acting right; which was often.

Drying her eyes, Teyanna let out a soft chuckle.

"Who knew you could be so sweet and caring." She joked, lightening the mood.

"Man, get the fuck out of here." He chuckled.

"What? I'm just saying."

"Me too. Yea, I know I ain't got no chill and I say some crazy shit sometimes, but I know how to treat a damn woman, ma." He told her as she continued to slightly, giggle.

"Nah, but for real, thank you." She looked up at him sincerely. "If it wasn't for you, ain't no tell what would have happened to me." She finished, fumbling with her fingernails.

"Look, ma. You ain't gotta thank me, I just did what was right. Don't no woman deserve to go through this shit. Especially one as beautiful as you." He told her, causing her to crack a smile.

"Okay, you going too far now. I haven't even seen myself and I know I look like shit." She stated, as the smile that graced her face disappeared. "I feel like I've been run over by a damn Metro bus." Teyanna pouted, sadly.

"Aye man chill out, I meant what I said. Those scares are just temporary; you gon overcome that. And when it's all said and done, you're still beautiful."

"Yea, well what about the way I feel on the inside. I'm broken, Byron, ain't no fixing that." She stated, as the tears slowly began to roll out, again.

Sighing deeply, Chubbz softly wrapped his arms around Teyanna, pulling her in close. He didn't know exactly the words to say, all he knew was he wanted to be there for her. He could tell that the tears she, were crying were tears of pain, and he wanted to take all of it away; she didn't deserve to hurt anymore.

"Everything can be fixed, babe. You just concentrate on healing yourself, leave that broken heart up to a real nigga like me." He whispered, as she softly whimpered in his chest.

Teynna had been through so much, she had finally reached her breaking point. She could only pray to God that Byron was her happily ever after.

∞∞∞

"Uhm, can I hold my baby now?" Fragile joked, as she watched Fatz bond with her newborn baby girl. He was standing by the big, hospital room window, as he rocked her tightly in his arms, whispering cute things to her.

"Nah, we chillin. Let a nigga have his moment, you'll have plenty of time with her." He told her. "Ain't that right stinka mama?!" He cooed, focusing his attention back on the baby.

"Oh, Gawd!" Fragile chuckled, leaning her head back against

the hospital bed, that she had sitting halfway up.

Emerald Jewel Banks was born 8 pounds 13 ounces, with a head full of coal black, curly hair. She was a spitting image of her mother, with her chinked eyes and cute button nose. Not to mention she was a chunky little thing. She was an angel already, being that she'd given her mother the smoothest delivery ever. Fragile didn't even have to get an epidural. When she and Fatz arrived at the hospital, to their surprise she was already crowning. After four strong pushes, baby Emerald made her grand entrance into the world; her mother didn't even break a sweat.

"I'm so glad I didn't have to get any drugs or stitches. I just knew her big head ass was gonna buss my pussy wide open." Fragile breathed a sigh of relief.

"You welcome." Fatz shot over his shoulder, as he continued to stare out of the window, rocking baby girl.

"What?" She scoffed.

"I said you're welcome."

"What's that supposed to mean?" She asked, wondering where the hell he was getting at.

"I'm the reason you had a smooth delivery." He told her.

"And how is that?" Fragile asked with a raised brow. Fatz smacked his lips.

"Come on now, don't play. You know how."

"Nah, I don't. So, enlighten me." She looked at him waiting for his reply.

"Girl don't sit over there and act like I wasn't droppin major, dick off in that pussy when that water broke. I knocked that thang LOOSE!" He laughed. Fragile quickly snatched the tissue box from the hospital table in front of her, and threw it at his head; Fatz ducked.

"Aye girl," He chuckled. "Don't be throwing shit while I got my baby. You could've accidentally hit her." He told her.

"Shut up, nigga! I can aim, I ain't gone hit MY baby." She flinched at him.

"With yo extra tough ass!" Fatz continued laughing.

"And stop cursing around my daughter, punk!"

"Hush! She don't understand what I be saying, yet."

"Yeah, whatever." She flipped him the bird.

"You still haven't talked to Byron?" Fragile then asked on a more serious note. "I've been trying to call Teyanna and she's not answering, that's not like her. She's going to fuckin flip when she finds out she missed the birth of her God daughter." She finished.

"Nah, I ain't talked to that ni.." Fatz paused in mid-sentence. "Aw, shit!" He then cursed himself.

"What?!" Fragile jumped, wondering what the matter was.

"I forgot to turn my damn phone back on. The nigga probably been trying to call me. Hell, if I know my brother, ain't no, probably." He told her.

Securing Emerald in his right, forearm, Fatz used his left hand to retrieve his phone from his pocket. Powering it back on, he waited for it to load then immediately called his brother.

"What the fuck bruh?! I been calling yo ass all fuckin morning. Where the fuck you at?" Chubbz barked, picking up on the first ring.

"I know, I know, my bad bro. I'm at the hospital with Fragile, she had the baby. I cut my phone off last night cause this bitch kept ringing and a nigga was tryna get his rocks off. When her water broke and shit it threw my mind off and I forgot to cut it back on. What's up? Where you at? Everything good?"

"Fuck nah, I'm up here at Mercy medical center emergency room."

"What?! For what?" Fatz asked anxiously.

"Don't say nothing, but I'm here with Teyanna. That punk

ass nigga of hers done beat her ass. I'm talkin bad, bro."

"What the fuck? How you get involved? Do we have to body a nigga?" Fatz asked, gritting his teeth.

"Nah, I mean, yeah eventually. I ain't worried about that nigga right now though. He bout still taking a nap from that ass whoppin I put on him anyway, but, I'm just trying to make sure Teyanna heals up iight."

"Yea, I feel that." Fatz shook his head. "Damn, that's fucked up. How she doing?" He then asked. He could see Fragile looking at him from the corner of his eye. He knew she was wondering what they were talking about.

"She finally woke up not too long ago. She's talking and joking and shit, but she fucked up. He did her ass bad. The nurse just came in and gave her some more pain meds, so I know she'll be back sleep in a minute."

"Aw, okay, okay." Fatz replied nodding his head.

"How's Fragile, smart mouth ass." Chubbz then asked.

"Aw, she good." He looked back at her and smiled. "Her delivery was easy and quick." He filled him in.

"Aw, I was hoping she would've had to get stitches all the way up to her ass crack." Chubbz replied, serious as fuck.

"What?!" Fatz bussed out laughing. "Nigga you a fool."

"Ole evil ass bitch!" He mumbled.

"Aye, watch ya mouth nigga!" Fatz told him.

"What he say?" Fragile blurted. She just knew Chubbz fat ass had said something smart about her; they stayed beefing. Fatz shook his head at her, as to tell her it was nothing.

"But, uhm we up here at Mercy in the Maternity ward." He continued his conversation.

"Cool, y'all in the same hospital we in. Man, please don't tell Fragile what's going on, I promised Teyanna I wouldn't say shit."

"Shiiit, I don't know how long that's gon last. She just had the baby, so you know how that go." Fatz tried speaking as low as possible, but Fragile was still all in his grill.

"Hell, yeah. She bout lookin for her ass right now."

"Ain't no bout, nigga. She is!" Fatz assured him.

"Fuck!" Chubbz sucked his teeth. "I don't know, man. Tell her we went on a lil mini vacay then."

"Iight, cool. I got you covered."

"Bet, thanks bruh."

"Always. Have a safe trip nigga." Fatz told him, sticking to the script. He then ended the call and pocketed his phone. Walking back over to Fragile's bed, he took a seat next to her.

"Sooo, what did he say?" She questioned.

"Oh, he said him and Teyanna up in the Ozarks. He took her phone, that's why she ain't been picking up."

Fatz felt like shit for lying. He wanted so badly to tell Fragile what was really going on but he didn't, for her sake. She had just given birth, so he didn't want her stressing. If circumstances were different he would have gladly told her, fuck what Teyanna and his brother were talking about. He felt it was wrong she was keeping some shit like that from her supposedly, best friend any damn way.

"What?! In the Ozarks?!" Fragile scoffed. "That bitch ain't told me shit! I can't believe she missed the birth of my baby to be up in the Ozarks with his fat ass!" She seethed; she was pissed.

As Fatz stared at the disappointment in her face, he began to feel worse. He didn't want her having a gripe against her friend over some stupid ass lie. Especially when the real reason she missed the birth of baby girl was out of her control. Yea he didn't want her stressing over Teyanna because she was hurt, but he really didn't want her pissed at her for no reason. Feeling like he was in a lose-lose situation he sighed deeply, running his hand over his face.

"Look man, we said we would keep it real with each other no matter what, and this shit ain't sitting right with me." He shook his head.

"Meaning?" She cocked her head to the side, letting him know she was all ears.

"Meaning, Teyanna and Chubbz ain't in no damn Ozarks, ma. They down in the emergency room." He confessed.

"In the emergency room?" Fragile's eyes got as big as saucers. "What they in the emergency room for? What kind of shit you and your gang banging ass brother got goin on that got them at the emergency room?!" She spat, assuming shit.

"Wait, wait, hold up. First of all, me and my brother ain't got shit goin on, so you can move the fuck around with all that assuming shit." Fatz barked, and Fragile got quiet as hell. "They down there because apparently Teyanna's punk ass boyfriend dun jumped on her and beat her up real, bad. They asked me not to tell you because they didn't want you to stress. At first, I thought it was a good idea not to tell you the truth, but seeing how disappointed you got when I said they were gone, I couldn't just let you be mad at her over a lie." He sucked his teeth.

"What?" Fragile stated in shock. "Quincy? What do you mean he beat her up?" She continued, looking clueless as ever.

"I didn't get all the details, but from what bro did tell me the pussy ass nigga did her bad. Don't trip though, we gon handle that. My word." Fatz assured her.

"Oh my God. Is she okay though, is she stable?" She asked worried.

"Aw, yeah. Bro said she up joking and talking. They came in and gave her pain meds, so she's about to get some rest and shit. He didn't say if they were keeping her or not, though. I'll find out."

"I have to get over there to see her." Fragile told him. Fatz looked at her ass like she was crazy.

"Aye, I don't mean no harm, but you ain't getting up and going nowhere yet."

"Bullshit! That's my friend, I need to go and see about her!" She protested.

"And I understand all of that, but you just pushed a whole baby up out yo twat, too. You need to sit yo ass down!"

"Boy, whatever. I feel fine." Fragile smacked her lips.

"I don't give a fuck what you FEEL, I said no. Shit still fresh and you need to let your body rest for a couple of days. Bruh got that on lock until you're able to move around. Just chill, relax and embrace being a new mother." He preached, causing Fragile to huff, and roll her eyes to the top of her head. Fatz chuckled as he got up from the bed.

"I don't give a fuck about none of that, you'll thank me later." He shot as he laid the baby in the little hospital cubby. Walking back over to Fragile, he placed a kiss onto her pouted, lips; her ass was really, mad. "I'll be back in a couple of hours." He then told her.

"Where you going?" She asked, still pissed.

"I'm bout to run to the crib and wash my nuts, then check on a few of my spots. I'll be back before you can miss me."

"Yeah whatever!" She scoffed.

"Man, stop actin like that." He told her giving her another kiss. "Fix your face, you too cute to be acting ugly." He chuckled.

"Fuck you!" Fragile flipped him the bird, trying her hardest not to crack a smile. It was so hard for her to stay mad at his, handsome, erky, fat ass.

"Nah, we gotta wait til that six weeks up." He shot back, heading for the door. Before exiting, he winked his eye and blew her a kiss.

Shaking her head, Fragile couldn't do shit but laugh. She couldn't stand his ass, yet she was falling in love with everything about him.

Chapter Four

Gangsta and pimps, Love lobsters and shrimps

Kool-Aid and chicken, Fancy things and women

All I need, is Remy and weed

Somebody not afraid, to co-sign for my Escalade

Gwahla pulled up into the driveway of Chief's residence bumping that old school Weezy, 500 Degreeze album. Throwing his black, 2018 GMC Denali truck into park, he shut off his engine and hoped out. Making his way to the door, he continued rapping the rest of the lyrics to the song, as he let himself inside of his deceased best friend's massive home. Stepping into the foyer, he closed and locked the door behind him before heading for the kitchen.

Throwing his keys onto the French, marble topped island, he felt a sense of anger come over him as he noticed wasn't any food cooking and the damn house looked a mess. There were dishes piled up in the sink and toys all over the floor. What the hell were toys doing in the kitchen any damn way, and where the hell was Zaria's lazy ass? Were the questions swarming his brain as he made his way to the refrigerator. Opening it up, he grabbed him a Modelo and closed it back up. Grabbing the bottle opener from one of the kitchen drawers, he popped the top off, before taking the beer to the head.

"Zaria!" Gwahla then called out after pulling the bottle of beer from his lips. Throwing the bottle opener onto the counter he made his was out of the kitchen, back down the long hall, to the spiral staircase. "Zaria where the fuck you at?" He looked towards the top as he sucked his teeth.

After still not getting an answer, he took it upon himself to go search for her. Once making up to the second level of the mini mansion, he headed straight for the master's suite that Marcus and Zaria had once shared but was now being occupied by them. When he made it in there he noticed clothes, shoes and suitcases, scattered all over the floor and California King sized bed. He heard coat hangers rambling inside of the walk-in closet, automatically assuring him where Zaria was. Sighing deeply, he sat his beer onto the nightstand and took a seat on the edge of the bed. A few seconds later, Zaria came storming out of the closet like a mad woman, just like he knew she would.

"What the fuck is this, Zaria? What are you doing?" He asked confused but calmly.

"What does it look like, Terrance? I'm packing!" She snapped, throwing the pile of clothes she had in her arms into the suitcase on the bed. Swiftly making an about face she tried heading back to the closet but was stopped by Gwahla grabbing her by the wrist, turning her back around to face him.

"To go where? Zaria this is crazy!"

"No, what's crazy is you going down to that fuckin police station and giving them a statement! Once this shit blows up, they're going to be looking for us to lock us the fuck up and I ain't sitting around waiting for that! I can't go to jail, Gwahla! What about my babies?" She looked him square in the eyes. "What about my kids?!" She yelled once more before breaking down.

Gwahla pulled Zaria in for an embrace. Running his fingers through her hair, she cried uncontrollably in his chest. Her mind was all over the place and she didn't know what to do next. She wished so badly that she could go back into the hands of time to undo what she and Gwahla had done, but she knew it was impossible. Her guilty conscience was beginning to get the best of her, and it was driving her insane. Yea Marcus had his flaws and she hated everything he had done to her, but she couldn't deny the fact that he didn't deserve to die. Every day she looked in her son's face, she got sick to her stomach just knowing that she had a hand in taking his father away from him for her own selfish reasons. How would she be able to forgive herself? She didn't think she would ever be able to.

"We're gonna be good, babe, I promise. Nothing can be traced back to us, I've told the police everything they need to know to make this all go away. You just have to be cool, sit back and wait. If we all of a sudden skip town, that will for sure raise antennas." He told her before planting a kiss on the top of her head.

"I'm so scared, Gwahla. What if shit doesn't go our way? I have a bad feeling about this. Something's telling me this shit is going to backfire and blowup in our faces." Zaria continued to sob. Roughly grabbing her by the shoulders, Gwahla broke them apart and began shaking her, expeditiously.

"Zaria, stop!" He barked causing her crying to abruptly cease. "Pull your fuckin self together! Stop thinking all of that negative shit! When you speak bad shit, bad shit happens! Now c'mon man, get it together. Breath and think positive thoughts. All that stressing you doing ain't good for my shorty." He finished as he placed his hand on her belly and began rubbing it. Zaria sighed deeply, running her fingers through her hair.

"Okay, maybe you're right. I just need to pull it together, everything's fine." She breathed in and out, trying to make herself believe those words as they left her lips.

"See, there you go. That's more like it. Just breathe, baby; everything is just fine."

Gwahla took Zaria by the hand and sat her down onto the bed. Sighing deeply, she rubbed her belly as she let out a slight chuckle.

"I guess I'm not the only one on edge, it feels like this little boy is using my insides as a damn jungle gym!" She slightly chuckled.

"Yea, that's because you're stressing him the fuck out. He don't know what the hell going on out here; all he hear his commotion." Gwahla sucked his teeth. Picking up his beer, he turned it up to his lips. Zaria scoffed, cutting her eyes at him.

"Hell, can you blame me?" She spat still rubbing her belly. It felt as if she was starting to have some contractions. Leaning forward, she winced in pain as she began to pant; taking short deep breaths in and out.

"Aye, you good?" Gwahla asked quickly sitting his beer down and running to her aid.

"Yea, I'm good. I'm just having some minor contractions. I gotta pee, though. Can you help he up so I can get to the toilet?" Zaria asked in a voice filled with pain.

"Yea, come on."

Grabbing her by the hand with one hand, Gwahla used his other hand to secure her by the elbow. They both counted to three before Zaria gave herself a slight push and Gwahla pulled her onto her feet.

"You good or you need me to walk to the bathroom with you?" He asked before letting her go.

"Nah, I should be fine. I just needed help getting up, all this damn belly!" Zaria sighed. "I'll call you, because I may need you to help me off of the toilet." She laughed before waddling off into the jointed bathroom. Gwahla just stood there watching as he laughed, shaking his head. Picking his beer back up, he took a seat on the edge of the bed and waited for her to come back out.

Once making it into the huge bathroom, Zaria made her way over to the toilet. As she began to pull her pink, Victoria Secret, sweats down she began to feel a sense of tightness at the bottom of her belly, causing her to double over in pain. Zaria sighed heavily as she rubbed her belly in a circular motion trying to ease the tension.

Come on Mori, just let mommy use the bathroom please.

Just as those words left her lips, she felt a flush of warm fluids leaking from between her thighs; drenching her pants, creating a puddle beneath her feet. Gasping in shock, she immediately began yelling out for Gwahla. He wasted no time coming to her aid.

"What's the matter, baby?!" He burst through the bathroom door, looking around frantically.

"I think my water broke!" She panted trying to practice her breathing.

"Are you serious?" He looked like a deer caught in headlights as he noticed the puddle of water at her feet.

"Nah, I'm joking." Zaria smacked her lips with sarcasm. "Yes, Terrence I'm serious! Don't you see all of this damn water!" She snapped.

"Okay, okay. I'm sorry." He panicked. "What you need me to do?" He asked confused as fuck. He didn't know what was next, it was his first baby and he'd never been in this predicament before.

"Oh my God, really Terrence?!" She huffed rolling her eyes to the top of her head.

This nigga is about as dumb as a doorknob, was all she could think as the contractions began to get worse. That was another thing that made her regret what they'd done. At least when she was in labor with her first son, Marcus knew what to do and how to keep her comfortable. All Gwahla knew how to do was stand there and look dumb as hell. She was so fuckin irritated she could punch him right in the face.

"Just get me some fresh pants, please! Can't you see that I'm wet!" Zaria yelled, causing Gwahla to dart out of the bathroom like a bolt of lightning.

Huffing in frustration, she removed the wet bottoms from her ass and began wiping herself up. In a matter of minutes

Gwahla returned with a pair of dry, grey Nike sweatpants and helped her put them on. Once she was finished, he cleaned up the water from the floor before they headed out of the bathroom, to get ready for their trip to the hospital.

"Don't forget to grab the baby bag, it's already ready." Zaria stated pointing at the black and white Mickey Mouse themed diaper bag that rested on the nightstand, as she slipped her feet into a pair of mint green, Rhiana Fenty slippers.

Snatching the bag, Gwahla quickly tossed it onto his shoulder before grabbing Zaria by the hand, escorting her out of the bedroom and down the steps. Before leaving out the door, she set her home security system and they made their way to her silver, 2018 Range Rover. Opening, up the passenger side Gwahla let her in, sitting the diaper bag on the floor underneath her feet. After closing her in, he ran to the driver's side and quickly let himself in.

"What hospital we going to?" He asked cranking up the engine.

"Mercy!" She replied between breaths, feeling her contractions getting closer.

Throwing the car in gear, Gwahla smashed on the gas sending the car forward, instead of in reverse like he'd intended to. Quickly slamming on the brakes he came to a sudden halt, just inches away from crashing into the garage.

"What the fuck, Terrence!" Zaria screamed damn near catching whiplash.

"I..I'm sorry, babe. I thought I put it in reverse." He stated in his defense. He was so damn nervous he didn't know whether he was coming or going.

"Don't be sorry muthafucka be careful! You almost ran us into the damn garage!" Zaria snapped hotter than a four hundred, pound bitch stranded in the Sahara, desert. "Damn, do I need to drive myself to the hospital to make sure we arrive in one fuckin piece?!" She asked serious as hell. She knew damn well she wasn't in the position to be operating a motor vehicle but by the looks of it, neither was he.

"Nah, man. Chill the fuck out, I got this. I'm just a little fuckin nervous, aiight!" He spat throwing the car in reverse; this time successfully backing out of the driveway.

"Well you need to get it together." She cut her eyes at him coldly. "QUICK!" She finished, slumping down in her seat.

She was pissed off and she could already tell that it was going to be a long, hard, frustrating delivery.

∞∞∞∞

"Oh Fragile, just look at her. She's just so precious; she looks just like you when you were this age!" Nana Banks gushed as she admired the beauty of her great grandbaby, who was swaddled in the crease of her arm. It was her first time seeing her and she was in awe of her cuteness.

"Yea, I couldn't deny her if I wanted to. All that hair explains why I had all that heartburn." Fragile chuckled a bit as she watched her grandmother bond with baby Emerald.

"That and all of those hot chips you were eating." Nana Banks shot back.

"Well I guess that contributed a little to it too." Fragile snickered. "Just a little bit." She finished, using her fingers to measure a tiny bit of air.

"A little bit? Girl you should be ashamed of yourself for those lies you telling. You ate those jokers every day you were pregnant with this baby and you gonna try to blame that heartburn on her? Shame on you!" Nana Banks playfully rolled her eyes at her granddaughter. "She got her nerves, don't she Nana baby?!" She cooed at baby Emerald as she rocked her lightly, walking around the spacious hospital room.

"Oooh now she's Nana's baby? Ain't that nothing, just knock me out of my spot, huh?" Fragile scoffed, raising her brow.

"Jealous much?"

"Nah, you just remember that when you need somebody to talk to. Emerald got a few years before she's able to talk back." Fragile sassed playfully.

"Aw hush, spoiled ass. You know you're still my baby. You're just my big baby and Emerald is my baby, baby." Nana Banks giggled.

"Yea, yea, don't try to butter me up now."

"No, I'm serious. You're my one and only grandchild, you will always be my baby." Nana Banks smiled at Fragile.

"Awwww Nana, you gonna make me cry!" Fragile fake sniffled. "I love you too." She then smiled.

"Oh, hush. Don't get too comfortable, now." Nana Banks cut her eyes at her granddaughter. "I'm still pissed you didn't call me when you were in labor." She smacked her lips in frustration.

Fragile huffed, tossing her head back against the hospital bed. "Really, Nana?! I thought we were past that." She huffed.

"We were, but I can't help but feel a certain way. You could've just called, Fragile, you knew how much seeing this baby being born meant to me." Nana Banks stressed.

"Yes, I know, Nana. But I told you, everything happened so fast. I didn't have time to call." Fragile repeated for like the thirtieth time.

Since her grandmother had walked through the door, she'd been fussing at her about not seeing the baby being born. Fragile had been trying to explain to her that it wasn't her intention not to call, it was just that with everything happening so fast, she couldn't think straight in that moment. Not to mention she went into labor while bouncing up and down on some good dick, and she damn sure couldn't tell her Nana that. She just honestly wished she'd let it go and enjoy her visit with her and Emerald. It could all be so simple.

"Yea, that's what you say." Nana Banks smacked her lips. "You had time to call that heathen!" She finished, rolling her eyes in disgust. Fragile couldn't do anything but shake her head, her grandmother was always jumping to conclusions.

"Really, Nana?" Fragile smacked her lips. "Brian is not a heathen, he's sweet. And I've already told you we were together when my water broke." Fragile rolled her eyes at her grandmother's back. She loved the fuck out of her Nana there was no denying that, but she really knew how to work a person's nerves.

"Sweet?" Nana Banks scoffed. "He looks like a little thug ass if you ask me. Dread locs all over his head, tattoos all over his face and body." She mentioned with the look of disgust. "And who the hell walks around town with no shirt on?! His little fat ass needs to be covered up; man breast and belly flapping all over the place!"

Fragile's mouth flew open, she couldn't believe her granny was really sitting in front of her roasting the fuck out of her boy toy. What did he ever do to her? Why was she so mad? Was all Fragile could think as she shook her head and giggled. The situation was far from funny, but she had to admit, Nana had jokes. She was just mad the jokes were on Brian. Which she couldn't understand because he'd been nothing short of respectful to Nana Banks. Granted they didn't see each other much because when he came around she was either sleep or gone to bingo, but when he did see her, he made it his business to speak. So, Fragile was lost on what the problem was.

"Nana why are you going so hard on my friend? You don't even know him like that." Fragile spoke in Fatz's defense.

"That's the point, I don't know him. And the boy just looks like trouble, Fragile. I don't trust him."

"Well, I do. He's been nothing but good to me and he's been a big help with Emerald. By the way, ain't your favorite saying *never judge a book by its cover?*" Fragile hit her grandmother with a line she used against her all the time when she was coming up.

"Are you tryna be smart, heffa?!" Nana Banks snapped her neck in her direction.

"Nooo, I'm just saying think about it. Perfect example, you loved the heck out of Marcus. You thought he was the most innocent man ever, just by the way he carried himself, when he was one of the biggest dope dealers out here! Even when you found out what he did for a living, you didn't want to believe it." Fragile pleaded her case.

Nana Banks stood there silent as she continued to rock baby Emerald in her arms. As much as she hated to admit it, Fragile was right. She loved Marcus; in her eyes he was perfect for Fragile and could do no wrong. It broke her heart when she found out from old friend, who happened to be related to Marcus, that he was on of St. Louis's most notorious dope boys. What shattered her heart, was when he died, leaving her granddaughter to mourn his absence.

"Okay, I have to admit you're right." Nana Banks replied after a brief, moment of silence. "But don't think for a second that you checkin me!" She finished. Fragile busted out laughing.

"Oh my God, Nana! Nobody is trying to check you; I just want you to give my friend a chance. He isn't anything like you think." Fragile told her.

"Yea, okay. We'll see, I'll be the judge of that." Nana Banks cut her eyes. "But, while we're on the subject of Marcus, when are you going to let his family know that he has another child out here? Don't you think they would want to know that?"

Fragile smacked her lips as she sighed deeply. Her grandmother just didn't know how to leave well enough alone! They'd just gotten done hashing out her issues with Brian and her delivery, now she was bringing up some more shit they'd already discussed. It was like Fragile couldn't catch a break. Like damn, she did just give birth to a whole baby! She wasn't even giving her time to rest before hitting her with bullshit she didn't care to talk about.

"Nana, please. I do not want to talk about this, AGAIN!"

"Well you're going to have to talk about it again, sooner or later. So why not right now, mhm? She looked Fragile square in the eyes. "Don't you think that child's mother would want to know that there's another piece of her son floating around here? That just might make her whole again." Nana Banks tried talking some sense into her stubborn ass grandchild. She couldn't understand for the life of her why she was being so damn bitter because she was sure as hell, she hadn't raised her to be that way.

"Well she's not the only piece of him floating around, so they good. They have his son and possibly another one on the way." Fragile snapped. She used the word *possibly* so loosely because judging by what she saw when she ran into Gwhala and Zaria at the store, there was no telling whose baby it was.

"I be damned if I be the girl to show up at Ms. Jefferson's doorstep, claiming to be her deceased son's baby mother." Fragile continued with attitude.

Noticing how annoyed her granddaughter was becoming, Nana Banks stayed silent and let the situation go. Trying to get Fragile to see the bigger picture was like beating a dead horse and she was over it. Taking a seat down in the rocking chair that rested in front of the huge hospital room window, she slowly rocked back and forth as she gazed out at the sunset.

Despite all, of the shit Fragile was talking, she knew she had to find a way to get information on the whereabouts of Ms. Jefferson; it was only right.

Chapter Five

"Excuse me, miss. May I please get another orange juice?" Detective Morales stopped the brunette, brown eyed, waitress that was about to pass their table.

"Sure, I'll go grab that for you. Will you like anything else?" She asked grabbing his empty glass.

"No, that will be all." Morales shook his head and the waitress pranced on her way to fulfill his request.

Morales and Harrington were at the Cracker Barrel on New Hallsferry Rd., having a quick bite to eat before hitting the streets again, to dig up more information about their case. It had been thirty-six hours since they'd gotten the piece of information, they needed from Gwahla so all they needed to do was tie up the rest of their loose ends.

"So, where to when we leave here?" Detective Harrington asked before taking a sip of his coffee.

"Well," Morales began to speak as he stuck his fork into his pancakes, a bit of his eggs then his sausage. "I was thinking we'd go have a chat with little miss, Fragile." He finished before sticking the fork full of food into his mouth.

"Okay," His partner replied in a *tell me more,* manner.

"I mean, Cook did say that she's now dating the man that killed her, supposedly at the time he was murdered, boyfriend. Like come on, the shit isn't fuckin rocket science. The picture is painted vividly that she set him up." Morales insinuated.

"Wait, now we don't know that just yet. Let's not jump to

conclusions." Harrington placed his coffee down. "All we have is a piece of information that was told to us by a friend MONTHS after the murder took place." He finished.

"So, what are you saying, you don't trust the information?" Morales asked shoving a piece of bacon in his mouth.

"I mean if we're being honest, no. I don't trust the information or the person that gave it to us." Harrington shrugged nonchalantly.

"Oh my Gosh, Harrington! Come on, are you serious?!"

"Dead." Detective Harrington looked his partner square in the face; he couldn't have been more serious.

"But, how can you say that though? It all makes sense!" Morales argued. Harrington scoffed before letting out a sarcastic chuckle.

"Yea, to you. The shit sounds like a bunch of made up mumbo jumbo, to me. I mean let's think logical here; what REAL friend knows who killed his so, called BROTHER and not give the person up until months later. If I knew who killed my long, time friend right after I'd just parted ways with him, I don't give a damn what the circumstances are, I'm speaking up." Harington stated before sticking a fork full of his steak and eggs into his mouth.

"Mhm, so what are you saying, you think he had something to do with it?" Morales asked with a blank expression.

"I'm saying we need to dot our I's and cross ALL, of our T's before we start making convictions. We can go and see the girlfriend but let's get her side of the story before we label her as a suspect." Harrington finished.

"Okay, your call." Morales stated taking the last bite of his meal. "By the way, where the fuck is this lady with my orange juice?!"

Harrington shrugged and they both fell out laughing.

∞∞∞∞

Fragile stood in the mirror of the hospital room, bathroom as she brushed her hair into a sleek bun. Baby Emerald was away in the nursery and Fatz had stepped out for a minute to handle some business, so she finally had time to shower and get a little time for self. Since the doctors had cleared her and she was able to walk around, she figured she'd walk to the intensive care unit to pay her bestie a visit. She was still at lost for words about Teyanna's situation and even more pissed that she'd keep a secret like that from her, but she couldn't dwell on that. Her main concern was making sure her friend would be okay physically and mentally. Only Lord knows how being abused could fuck up a woman's head.

Exiting the bathroom with her dirty clothes in hand, Fragile grabbed a plastic bag that the hospital had provided and placed her clothes inside. Tying the bag up, she placed it in the bottom drawer across from the bed and closed it up. Grabbing her cellphone from the charger, she exited the room for the nurse's station. After letting them know that she would he away from her room for a while, she made her way to the other side of the hospital to visit Teyanna.

It took her all of five minutes to make it to the intensive care Unit. Stopping at the first desk she saw, she asked for Teyanna's room number. Once getting the information she needed, she walked down the hall to the first room on the right; the door was cracked so she tapped lightly.

"Come in." She heard her friend say just above a whisper.

Slowly pushing the door open Fragile quietly crept into the room, being sure to push the door back slightly closed. Tiptoeing around the corner of the doorway, the smile that graced her face suddenly disappeared as she took a good look at her friend.

"Oh my God, bestie!" Fragile cupped both hands over her mouth as tears began to form in the corners of her eyes.

She knew that her friend was hurt but she didn't think it was that bad. She was bandaged up just about everywhere and her face was practically beaten to a pulp. Fragile could barely stomach to see her friend in such state but she wouldn't dare leave her alone. Teyanna needed her and by her side she would stay; at least as long as she could.

"How are you feeling?" Fragile asked as she made her way to her friend's bedside. Leaning in, she placed a soft kiss onto her forehead, being sure not to hurt her in any way.

"Like I look." Teyanna scoffed with attitude.

Part of her was happy to see her best friend, but the other part was angry and embarrassed for Fragile to see her that way. For the longest she'd kept what she had been going through from her friend and she was doing it well. In Fragile's eyes Teyanna had always been the strong one; the one who held things together when either of them were going through. The last thing she wanted was to be labeled weak in Fragile's eyes, because that's exactly what she was for Quincy's bitch ass, weak. She hated that shit.

"Why didn't you just call me?!" Fragile suddenly burst into tears.

On the walk to the intensive care Unit she had given herself a pep talk and promised that she would keep her composure no matter how bad things were but seeing her bestie all banged up and bruised did something to Fragile's soul. Her friend was the sweetest of the sweet and she didn't deserve an ounce of what she was going through. How dare that punk ass nigga beat up on her friend like she was some random ass person on the street. Fragile was hot! She had never wished death upon anyone but the way she was feeling, she prayed Quincy got put out of his misery.

"Why would he do this to you? How long has he been doing

this?!" Fragile asked as the tears continued to pour down her face.

Looking directly up at the ceiling Teyanna stayed silent. She couldn't even look at her friend, let alone find the words to say to her.

"Teyanna please, talk to me." Fragile cried.

"What do you want me to say, Fragile?!" Teyanna snapped not really meaning to.

Her anger wasn't with her bestie, she was just ashamed. Ashamed that she'd let shit get so far that she was laid up in a hospital bed, fucked from head to toe. Nevertheless, it wasn't Fragile's fault. So, as a good friend and sister she did owe her as much as an explanation. Taking a deep breath, tears began to taint Teyanna's face as well.

"It was never supposed to get this bad, bestie. I wanted so bad to tell you; I swear I did. But I didn't know how!" She cried uncontrollably. "For our entire friendship I've always been the strong one. How was I supposed to tell you that my tough ass was getting my ass beat? We talk about bitches that condone this type of shit!" She scoffed feeling even more embarrassed as the words left her lips.

Fragile sighed deeply as she softly shook her head. As bad as she wanted to curse her friend the fuck out for keeping this secret from her, she couldn't blame her. She and Teyanna had always talked about different relationship scenarios and they'd always vowed to never be the battered woman. They didn't give a fuck how hard life got; they weren't sticking around for no ass whippings from no nigga. The day shit started getting physical would be the day they would be catching one of two things, a case or a body! Guess it was safe to say you never knew what the hell you would do until you were in that situation. Teyanna's predicament was a perfect example of that.

"You can't always be the strong one, T." Fragile took a softer approach as she rubbed the back of her friend's hand. "Sometimes

I have to be the shoulder for you to lean on. We all have weak moments and we all go through things we say we'd never go through. That doesn't mean we're weak individuals, it means we're human. No one is exempt from anything; it could be me laying in this bed. I can't say that I don't feel some type of way about you not telling me, I mean how can I not. You're my best friend, T; the closest thing I'll ever have to a sister. It breaks my heart to see you like this, but, I would be lying if I said I didn't understand why you never said anything. Just know for future reference, you can come to me about anything; and I mean anything. I will never judge you; I don't care what it is, T. I will always be here to have your back and pick up the pieces. I love you best friend!" Fragile cried as she poured her heart out to Teyanna.

"I love you too, bestie." Teyanna looked down as she fumbled with the cast that covered her left, hand to secure her broken fingers. She couldn't even look at her bestie she felt so disconcerted. "Now I feel like a bad friend." Teyanna huffed trying to stop the tears.

"Please, don't because a bad friend is something you've never been." Fragile expressed as she softly ran her fingers through her friend's hair. "Seriously I can imagine how hard it was for you to tell me, even though I don't know how I missed the signs. I should be the one feeling like the bad friend." Fragile stated as a flush of guilt run through her heart.

She and Teyanna had been friends for years and they knew one another like the back of their hands. If one was going through something the other could definitely feel it. So, she couldn't understand how the shit got past her without warning.

"To be honest bestie, I hid the shit too fuckin well. You would have never guessed unless I told you, but, you should have known I wasn't trying to be no damn makeup artist. Even though I am kind of good at the shit." Teyenna scoffed confessing the lie she'd told her bestie the day they were on the way to her first doctor's appointment. Since she was being honest, she figured she may as well tell the whole truth. Fragile cut her eyes at her friend as she smacked her lips.

"You, fuckin bitch! You shol fuckin right, I don't know why I fell for that shit!" She shoved her friend in the shoulder.

"Owww bitch! Did you forget where we are!" Teyanna winced in pain.

"Oooh, I'm so sorry. I'm so sorry!" Fragile honestly didn't mean to shove her that hard. She honestly did forget where they were just that fast.

"Yea, whatever bitch, you did that on purpose. I guess I deserved that though, so I'll take it." Teyanna slightly chuckled.

"No, I promise I didn't. I would never intentionally hurt you, friend. You know way better than that." Fragile replied sincerely.

"Yea, yea, I know I'm just kidding." Teyanna continued snickering. "Well, enough about me, let's talk about you and my new God daughter! How is she?!" Teyanna asked excitedly. Even though she was down bad, she refused to be in anything but good spirits. Good energy was good for the soul; plus, it would help her through a speedy recovery.

"She's great! I knew you would ask about her, so I brought my phone down to show you pictures." Fragile gushed as she unlocked her phone and pulled up the picture's she'd taken of baby Emerald. There were so many, so she just placed the phone in Teyanna's right hand and let her scroll through them all herself.

"Oh my God, friend, she's so beautiful!" Teyanna beamed at the pictures in awe, as the tears she managed to stop, began to slowly return down her cheeks. "I know you don't want to hear this, but she looks just like her damn daddy. Wooow, I wish he was here to see this. This shit is crazy!" She finished.

"Girl, bye. She looks like me, even my nana said it. And he sees her, I know he does. When my baby is sleeping, all she does is smile and coo. Two days old and she's already cooing; I know it's because he's playing with her in her dreams." Fragile stated as she thought about her late boyfriend.

Even though she tried her best not to think about him, she couldn't help but to wonder how things would've been if Marcus was still alive. A daughter was something he'd always wanted so she knew baby Emerald would've been his pride and joy. As she smiled at Teyanna flipping through the images of their baby girl, a lone tear managed to escape her eye. She quickly wiped it away.

"Man, she's so beautiful! I can't wait to hold her!" Teyana expressed smiling from ear to ear.

"I know right! I wish I could've brought her with me to see you, but you know how that go." Fragile smacked her lips.

"Yeah, I do." Teyanna nodded. "Her too small, yes her is!" She cooed at the phone while looking at the last few pictures. When she got to the end, she handed Fragile back her phone.

"Yeah, she is." Fragile grabbed the phone from her friend's grasp. "You shouldn't be in here too much longer, so you'll see her soon." She finished pulling up a chair to her friend's bedside, taking a seat.

"Yea, hopefully." Teyanna sighed, dryly.

"Awww bestie don't act like that, I'm positive they won't keep you long." Fragile grabbed her friend's good hand and gave it a slight squeeze.

For about an hour and a half, Fragile sat with her bestie and they had good conversation, before it was time for her to get back up to her room and check on baby Emerald. She shared with her how Nana Banks felt about her telling Marcus's mother about the baby, all while expressing how she felt about the situation also. She was a bit salty when her bestie sided with her grandmother, but she was still standing firm on her opinion. What the Jefferson's didn't know couldn't hurt them, and they didn't know about baby Emerald.

As far as Fragile was concerned, it would stay that way.

∞∞∞

Nana Banks sat at her dinning, room table with her head buried in her laptop as she created her a Facebook account. She wasn't computer literate by far, so she had been sitting there awhile trying to figure it all out. Usually Fragile would be there to help her in situations like this but since she was still admitted in the hospital, Nana had to do it all on her own. Besides, she didn't want her granddaughter to know what she was up to anyway. If she found out, she would surely be pissed.

After finally entering all, of the information in for her profile, her account was finally set up. She made sure to use a fake name and a picture of Michelle Obama, just in case her page happened to pop up in anyone's *people you may know* section. Nana wasn't a fan of social media, so she didn't need anyone to know she had a profile. All, of her good girlfriends had one, but she wasn't into all that. If she wanted to reach out to someone, she would rather do it the old-fashioned way; by phone or visit. Nana Banks was making a page for one reason, and she was going to use it for that reason only.

Putting her cursor into the search engine, Nana typed in the name *Minetta Jefferson.* Saying a small prayer, she hit search hoping that Marcus's mother owned a Facebook page. She silently gave thanks to God as several Minetta Jefferson's popped up and the very first one had a profile picture of Marcus's obituary. It was obvious it had to be his mother's page, so Nana immediately clicked on it, going to her photos. After taking a look at them, she was certain she had the right profile. There were photos from when Marcus was little, up to his funeral repast; not to mention he and his mother were damn near identical.

Backing out of the photo section, she went back to Ms. Jefferson's timeline and continued browsing. Her heart began to ache as she read some of the statuses and looked at all the pictures she'd been sharing, in memory of her son. She could tell that her wounds were still fresh, and she was missing her child daily. Just by looking at her most recent selfies, she could see the hurt in her eyes. Nana Banks couldn't imagine that kind of pain. If something were to happen to her dear Fragile, she wouldn't be able to take it. Only Lord knows how she would react.

Scrolling back up to the top of the page, Nana banks clicked the message button. Sighing deeply, she quickly got her thoughts together as she prepared herself for what she was about to send.

Hello,

I'm sorry to bother you. I know you don't know me, but my name is Margaret Banks. My granddaughter, Fragile Banks, and your son were dating before he passed and I am reaching out because I will like to meet with you so that we can speak. There is something you need to know, something that just may bring your dark nights to days again. If it's not too much to ask, can you please give me a call at 314-227-7997. I hope to hear from you soon.

Nana Banks read over her message before hitting send. Logging out of the anonymous Facebook account, she cleared any trace of the site. Fragile often used her laptop for schoolwork and the last thing she needed was for her to stumble upon her dirty work. Once she was certain that everything was gone, she powered off the Mac book and closed it up. Getting up from the table, she took it and placed it back in its usual spot.

Ding-Dong!

Just as she was about to head up the steps to take her a nap before midnight bingo, she heard the doorbell. Making an about face to head for the door she wondered who it could be, being that she wasn't expecting anyone. Making sure to tread lightly, she quietly crept to the door. Peeking out of the blinds, she noticed two men dressed in suits; one African American, the other Mexican. She hadn't seen neither of them a day in her life, so she didn't know who they were or why the hell they were at her doorstep.

"Who is it?!" Nana asked through the door with a bit of aggression.

"St. Louis Metropolitan Police department." The Mexican one flashed his badge in front of the peephole.

St. Louis Metropolitan police? Nana Banks said to herself as she tried to figure out why they were at her home. It wasn't any emergency there so she damn sure hadn't called them. Not to mention they weren't your average blue shirt cops; they were detectives, and that alone made Nana nervous. Unlatching the locks, she quickly swung open the door. Looking the two up and down, she folded her arms across her chest and leaned against the door frame.

"How may I help you?" She then asked seriously.

"Good evening ma'am." The African American one spoke up. "Sorry to bother you, but we're looking for a Fragile Banks. Would she happen to be here?" He asked slyly looking around her, trying to get a peek inside.

"Who wants to know?" Nana shot back curiously. How dare they come to her house asking for her grandchild without stating their names and the reason for their visit.

"I'm detective Harrington and this is my partner detective Morales." He looked over at his partner as he introduced him. Morales gave a slight smile and a quick wave.

"And, why are you here looking for my grandbaby might I ask?" Nana Banks wasn't moved by the introduction. She just wanted them to get to the reason they were there, already.

"Well," Detective Harrington slightly chuckled as he overlooked her obvious attitude. "my partner and I are working the case of Marcus Jefferson and we would like to ask her a few questions, if you don't mind." He finished hoping he would be able to speak to Fragile, after bypassing her security.

"The case of Marcus Jefferson?" Nana Banks scoffed. "That boy was shot down months ago and to my understanding my grandbaby has told y'all everything she knows about that night. Please don't come to my home pouring salt on an open wound. My child has been through ENOUGH! She just gave birth to a baby and she doesn't need this extra stress. Now will you please excuse me, I was just going to bed!" Nana snapped turning to close her door, but before she could, Detective Morales stuck his foot in the door. Nana Banks quickly shot him a menacing glare. If looks could kill, he would have definitely been DOA.

"Listen, ma'am. Your granddaughter could be in serious, danger. She is involved with some really, dangerous people. We just need to speak with her to make sure she doesn't go down with them." Morales explained hoping she would calm down and listen. Just as he expected, Nana Banks opened the door back up and was suddenly interested in what they had to say.

"Dangerous people? What people?" She asked with fear and concern written all over her face, trying to figure out what he was insinuating. Detective Harrington immediately intervened, giving Morales the side eye.

"What my partner is trying to say is, we have some new leads on Jefferson's case. Someone has come forward with a great piece of information and we need to speak with Fragile to get her side of the story before labeling her as a suspect." Harrington explained.

"Suspect?!" Nana gasped in shock. "Are you trying to accuse my Fragile of being involved in Marcus's murder?!" She placed her hand on her chest.

"No. What I'm trying to say is, with the new information we have, we need to rule out anyone that was with Mr. Jefferson the night he was murdered. Now, is there a chance you'd like to tell us where your granddaughter is?" Harrington asked giving her another chance to tell them what they needed to know.

Nana Banks sighed deeply as she gave it some thought. She wanted so badly to tell the two pigs to kiss her ass and get the fuck off, of her porch, but something in her gut was telling her to cooperate. Though she didn't know what was going on, the last thing she wanted was to make matters worse for Fragile. The situation was serious, so if all they wanted to do was ask questions, she would let them.

"She's in Mercy medical center out there off Ballas Road; Sixth floor." Nana finally gave in. "She's supposed to be discharged tomorrow, but she hasn't had a bowel movement, so they won't let her go until she has one." She finished dryly.

"Do you have a room number?" Morales asked whipping out his notepad and pen. He instantly began to jot down the information.

"6208."

"Thank you so much, ma'am. I promise you you're doing the right thing." Harrington told her as he reached out for a handshake. Nana Banks was a bit hesitant but reluctantly shook his hand.

"Just questions, right?" She then asked regretfully.

"Just questions. I promise." Harrington smiled with honesty as his partner flashed a devilish grin.

"We'll be in touch." He stated sliding the notepad and pen back into his suit jacket. He too then extended his hand for Nana to shake, but she declined. It was something about that muthafucka that she just didn't like. He was dirty, and she could smell his bullshit from a mile away.

"Well," Morales chuckled once he noticed she wasn't going to shake his hand. "you have a nice night." He told her before turning to leave her doorstep.

"We'll be in touch ma'am." Harrington gave a warm smile before following his partner.

Going back into the house, Nana closed her door and locked it up. Placing her back against it, she sighed deeply as she said a silent prayer, asking God to cover her grandbaby through whatever was going on. Out of all, of her 23 years of living, she'd never known Fragile to be in any trouble and she didn't want her to start.

Interrupting her prayer, Nana heard her phone began to ring from her bedroom. Taking off towards the staircase, she darted up the steps to retrieve it. Snatching it from the nightstand, she noticed an unsaved number flashing across her screen. Though it was unfamiliar she answered anyway.

"Hello," Nana was still trying to catch her breath.

"Hi, will there happen to be a Margaret Banks available?" An elderly woman spoke through the phone. Pulling the phone from her ear, Nana looked at it as if it would help her recognize the voice.

"Uhm, this is she. May I ask who you are?" She questioned after placing it back up to her ear.

"Yes, my name is Minetta, Minetta Jefferson."

∞∞∞

"What the hell was that?!" Detective Harrington seethed as he and his partner made their way to their vehicle.

"What the hell was what?" Morales questioned with a slight chuckle.

"Don't fuck with me, Morales. You know exactly what I'm talking about." Harrington shot back as he swung open the passenger door to their 2016 Chevy Impala. Flopping down into the seat, he slammed the door behind him.

"Buddy, relax. I was just doing my job. She told us what we wanted to know didn't she?" Morales said once jumping into the driver's and closing himself in. Sticking the keys into the ignition, he cracked up the car and pulled away from Nana Banks' place.

"There are better ways to get answers from people without making them feel uncomfortable. You had that poor lady scared to death! We don't even know if her granddaughter even has, a hand in this; she could be completely innocent!" Harrington stressed. He was past irritated with his overly aggressive ass partner. After all, they were working off, of word of mouth and he was acting as if they had cold, hard evidence.

Yea, well right now everyone is guilty until proven innocent in my book." Morales scoffed, pulling off from a red light. "You just need to get your head in the game and get with the program." He finished.

"What the hell is they supposed to mean?" Harrington grimaced snapping his neck in Morales's direction.

"Exactly what I said." Morales took a quick look at his partner from the corner of his eye before focusing his attention back on the road.

Harrington remained silent as he stared out of the passenger window. There was so much more he wanted to say, but he knew it was better left unsaid. He could talk until he was blue in the face, but it still wouldn't make his partner see things his way. Honestly, he was sick of it. 22 years with the St. Louis Police Department, Harrington had been a detective for 12. Out of all the cases he'd been put on, he had solved all but 9; and that didn't start until Morales had become his partner. Clearly the shit wasn't just a coincidence. Morales was bad luck and his fucked, up attitude and nonchalant demeanor, was a big part in why most of their cases went cold. Harrington wasn't having it with Jefferson's case though. Yes, there was definitely a culprit, but for some strange reason, he knew it wasn't Fragile Banks.

"I don't think we should go visit miss Banks while she's in the hospital." Harrington finally broke the silence.

"What?! Come oooon!" Morales slapped the steering wheel. "Are you serious?!"

"Very. The child just gave birth for Christ's sake! To a dead man's baby at that." Harrington debated.

"You don't know that. After all, it could be the man's that murdered Marcus Jefferson in cold blood!"

"Oh, here you go!" Harrington waved his partner off. "Either way, I don't think we should go questioning her at the moment." He finished.

"So, what do you suggest, genius?!" Morales stated sarcastically.

"Are you being funny?" Harrington cut his eyes at him.

"Noooo," Morales chuckled. "I'm just asking since you don't think going to question one of our main suspects is a good idea." He was being even more sarcastic.

"I didn't say that it wasn't a good idea, I said it's not a good time." Harrington replied with irritation.

"Oh yeah, big difference." Morales made a goofy face, rolling his eyes to the top of his head.

"You know what, Morales? You can just drop me off back at the station because I have had enough of this sarcasm, bullshit!" Harrington seethed. "Fuckin narcissistic, asshole!" He finished focusing his attention back out of the window. He was pissed.

Morales instantly fell into a pit of laughter; he loved getting under his partners skin. Harrington wore his heart on his sleeve, and he hated that shit. He sympathized with everyone, even the suspects. Morales felt in the field they were in, there was no room for sympathy. His only concern was bringing justice to the victim's families and move on to the next case. It was sad to say, but he was one of those who only cared about a check.

"Alright, man. Take it easy, I was just fuckin around..." Morales continued to chuckle.

"Yea, well you fuck around a little too much." Harrington sucked his teeth.

"Damn man, I apologize." Morales placed his hand over his heart pretending to seem sincere. "I didn't think you would get so pissed.

"Yea, whatever. Like you care." Harrington scoffed.

The car fell silent for a moment as Morales continued to cruise down the boulevard. As much as he wanted to continue being a dick, he just couldn't find it in him. Truth be told, he wanted to solve Jefferson's case just as bad as Harrington did. He was tired of being labeled as the case flopper around the precinct. So, if it meant putting his pride to the side to get shit done, he was down to do that.

"No, but really, what do you think we should do next." Morales asked seriously, breaking the silence. Noticing that his partner was actually being serious for once, Harrington decided to kill the tension.

"I think we should go pay the Myer brother's a visit." Harrington replied.

"Now you talkin!"

Morales smiled whipping a you turn in the middle of the street.

Chapter Six

"Ayyyye, man! Look at you! Look at you, you look just like daddy! Yes, you do!"

Zaria looked on in disgust as Gwahla talked to their new-born son. After 12 hours of hard labor and no help from his green ass father, she had finally given birth to a handsome, bright eyed eight, pound baby boy. Unfortunately, he was a spitting image of Gwahla and it made Zaria sick to her stomach. Mainly because she knew it was getting closer to the time for her to face the music. There was no way she would be able to keep her secret now; one look at Mori Romell Grimshaw, and it was evident who his father was.

"Damn, bae, I can't believe I'm someone's father!" Gwahla beamed at Zaria with excitement.

"Yea, me neither." She replied dryly putting on a fake smile.

Zaria was trying so hard to appear okay on the outside, when deep down she was completely disgusted with herself. What she really wanted to say was, she couldn't believe she'd made him a father. She questioned herself every day on how she'd let her emotions sway her to be so wicked and disloyal. If only she could turn back the hands of time, she would have fixed the issues between she and Marcus and things would be okay. Despite what he had done, she was supposed to hold shit down and stay on top of her game. Instead she did the exact opposite. Zaria felt dirtier than dirty; ashamed to have even stooped so low.

"So, you know Mama Jefferson is on her way up here. She's bringing MJ to meet his brother." Zaria informed Gwahla hoping that would push him to cut his visit short and get the hell out of dodge. The last thing she needed was for Marcus's mother to show up and he was still there chilling, all comfortable. That would for sure raise her antennas, and she didn't need that at the moment. Zaria planned on coming clean, but she wanted to do it her way, on her terms.

"And?" Gwahla snarled shooting Zaria an evil glare, as he continued to rock their son in his arms.

"And, I think you should leave before they get here." She replied quickly.

"I'll leave when I get ready, I'm bonding with my son." Gwahla sucked his teeth. Focusing his attention back on the baby, he began talking to him again. Zaria scoffed rolling her eyes.

"No, I think you should go now. Terrence why do you have to be so difficult when you know what it is?!" She snapped.

"Yea, you right. I do know what the fuck it is!" Gwahla snapped, turning to face Zaria. "You my bitch and this my fuckin son!" He seethed pointing from her to the baby. "So, it seems like you the one that don't know what the fuck it is!" He finished.

"Here you go! We've fuckin talked about this!"

"Nah, you talked about this; everything is your fuckin way! When all I vividly remember is you riding this dick every night, begging for shit to be this way! Now since shit dun got real you wanna change on a nigga?! This is my baby, Zaria. MINE!" He screamed.

"Oh my God, really?!" Zaria scoffed looking around. "Keep your fuckin voice down!" She hissed. They were in the maternity ward of the hospital and his ass wanted to act a plum fool. Not to mention her room was right across from the nurse's station. The last thing she needed was them all in their business.

Gwahla looked around apologetically. He was so pissed he'd forgotten that they were even inside of the hospital. Walking over to the door, he cracked it open and stuck his head out. Looking both ways down the hall, he checked to make sure no one had heard them. Everyone seemed to have been minding the business that paid them, so he closed the door back, quietly.

"Look, I'm tired of hiding the truth." Gwahla used his inside voice as he made his way back over to Zaria's bedside. "Either you woman up and tell mama Jefferson the truth, or I'm taking my baby and we're getting the fuck out of dodge. Your choice." He stated handing baby Mori back over to her. Zaria smacked her lips and rolled her eyes.

"Nigga you got me all the way fucked up! If you think ima just let you up and take my son away from me you're crazy as hell!" She snapped. If looks could kill, Gwahla would have been one dead nigga. Scoffing, he sucked his teeth and let out a slight chuckle.

"Yea, aight. You heard what the fuck I said, I'm out. When I come back, you should be telling me how shit went." He said meaning every word. Little did he know, Zaria didn't give a fuck about shit he was talking about. She had already told his ass that she would take care of it when she was ready, and that's exactly what the fuck she meant.

"Yea whatever, Terrence. Bye!" She put emphasis on the word bye, basically demanding him to get the fuck out.

Flashing her a cold glare, Gwahla shook his head and made his way toward the door. Opening it up he prepared to leave, but not before looking back at Zaria.

"Ignorant bitch!" He grimaced before walking out; he was pissed.

Storming his way through the long hospital halls, Gwahla made his way to the elevators. Upon approaching them, he pressed the downward arrow and waited for the elevator car to arrive. Sighing deeply, he ran his hands over his freshly, corn-rowed locs. He couldn't wait until he got to his whip so he could roll him up a fatty and ease his mind.

Bing!

Breaking him from his stressful thoughts, the elevator sounded, alerting him that the car had arrived at his floor. When the elevator doors opened, he breathed a sigh of relief once noticing the car was empty. The Lord himself knew when his attitude was on ten, he didn't need to be around general population.

Stepping onto the elevator Gwahla pushed the number one, for the first floor. Leaning with his back up against the wall, he hung his head and began shaking it in shame. For the first time since Marcus's murder he'd began to feel a little remorse for what he'd done. All their lives Marcus had been nothing short of loyal to him and in return he'd betrayed him; over some power and a piece of mediocre ass pussy at that. If Gwahla could turn back the hands of time, he would have never set his one and only friend up to be killed, and he damn sure wouldn't have fell into Zaria's manipulative web. It was too late for all the, should have, would have and could haves though; the damage was already done. He couldn't bring his dog back no matter how much he wanted to and that fucked with his mental, every day.

Bing!

The elevator doors opened. Gwahla was so caught up in his thoughts, he didn't realize he'd made it down to the first floor.

"Look, Granny! I told you that was his spaceship outside!"

He heard a small, familiar voice, causing his head to spring up from the floor. His stomach dropped to his feet and he felt a lump form in his throat, as his buked eyes landed on MJ and Moma Jefferson.

"Yea, you did." Ms. Jefferson stated to MJ but was staring dead at Gwahla. "Terrence, good to see you." She forced a smile.

"Hey, mama." He kissed her cheek. "What's up, lil man!" He smiled slapping fives with MJ. Taking his knuckles, he playfully dug them in the top of his little, skull; something he normally did. He was playing it cool as hell on the outside but was scared as hell on the interior.

"Haven't heard from you in a few days." She told him, studying his body language.

Ms. Jefferson and Gwahla hadn't communicated since the evening she'd called him over to her home to tell him the news regarding Marcus's will. Which was odd because since his passing, he'd made sure to stop by or at least call to check up on her. He hadn't done either. To make matters worse, the detectives had informed her of him changing his statement, and not once had he mentioned it to her. He was like a son to her, why wouldn't he tell her? Not to mention the little tea her grandson had spilled over breakfast one morning! That had her mind past, boggled.

"Yea, I know, ma. Please forgive me, I promise it's not intentionally." Gwahla sighed deeply. "I'm still dealing with the loss of my boi, all while tryna find some work. Working for Marcus all those years, I never needed a real nine to five. Since he's gone, things have been tough. I gotta find a way to keep the bread and butter flowing, ya know." He finished.

Gwahla had never taken a drama class a day in his life, but he was damn sure one hell of an actor. Little did he know, Ms. Jefferson wasn't moved by his performance. She wasn't a dummy by far. Even though her son tried to hide his street dealings from her, she very well knew he was in the streets. She also knew that Terrence was right there with him. Anything her son did, you better believe he had done it as well. Therefore, she knew he was well taken care of. So, who did he think he was fooling talking about a damn nine to five?

"Well in that case, I understand, son." She gave another half, smile. Since he thought she was dumb, she figured she'd play it. "So, what brings you here? Where are you coming from?" She asked curiously.

"O..oh, I was just leaving Zaria." He stated honestly.

"Oh, really?" She asked raising her left brow in suspicion.

"Y..yea, she ain't tell you?" He nervously chuckled. His eyes danced around as he quickly thought of a lie. "She had called me to drop off some food for her last night and when I got there, her water broke. I had to bring her here. I stayed until I felt she was good and now I'm leaving." He told half the truth.

"Oh, okay." Ms. Jefferson cleared her throat. "Well, that was nice of you."

"Yea, I mean, she's my best friend's girl. After all, he did make me Godfather. Ain't that right, MJ." Gwahla replied while reaching out to tickle MJ's tummy. He instantly bussed out in a giggle fit.

"That's right, uncle T!" He smiled brightly.

"My man!" Gwahla then gave his little fist some dap.

"Well, I guess we better get going so this boy can see his mama and I can see my new granny baby!" Ms. Jefferson gloated. She was so excited to have a new addition to the family. Especially since her son had gone on to glory. She felt like she had another little piece of him.

"I'll see you soon?" she asked with a raised brow as if she was asking, more so than telling.

"Yes, mama. You will see me soon." He smirked.

"Alright." She gave a fake chuckle. "Well, be safe out here." She then told him before pressing the upward arrow for the elevator.

"You too." He replied giving her another peck on the cheek and MJ another high five.

"Bye, uncle T!" MJ waved his free hand. The other was occupied in his grandmother's grasp.

"See you later, lil man."

Ms. Jefferson and MJ disappeared off onto the elevator as Gwahla walked away inhaling, and exhaling, deeply. He had again dodged another bullet.

∞∞∞

Ms. Jefferson exited the elevator at her designated floor as she held the hand of her overactive, grandson. She was so caught up in her thoughts, she was totally disregarding all, of the hopping, skipping, jumping and beat boxing he was carrying on. Her mind was flooded with all kinds of thoughts that she just couldn't shake, from the inbox she'd received from Nana Banks, to the bullshit ass lie Gwahla had just told her to her face; it was all just becoming too damn much.

As much as she hated to admit it, it was a bunch of fishy shit going on and the more she looked deeper into it, the more Gwahla bit the bait on her fishing pole. She wanted so badly to just let him know everything she knew, hoping he would come clean about it all, but that was too much like right. Gwalah would never come clean to her about being affiliated with the murder of her son, so she would continue to conduct her own investigation until she got all, of the information she needed. She was a firm believer in the saying, *what's done in the dark, always comes to light.* Whatever it was he was hiding he couldn't hide it forever and she was sure of that.

Upon making it to Zaria's room, Ms. Jefferson snapped out of her thoughts and gave the slightly closed, door a light tap. Before anyone could respond, MJ pushed the door open and invited himself in.

"Mommy, it's meeeee!" He announced, running in like he'd been there before. Quickly running after him Ms. Jefferson shook her head in shame.

"Boy, get back here!" She chuckled.

By the time she made it to him, he was already at his mother's bedside, staring down at his baby brother, who was swaddled in her arms. Ms. Jefferson smiled as she looked on in awe; he was so precious. He didn't look anything like MJ did when he was born, she couldn't deny that, but nevertheless he was handsome.

"What's his name?" MJ whispered smiling from ear to ear.

Zaria smiled as she looked over at him. "His name is Mori." She told him. "Say hi to Mori, pooh."

"Hi, Mori." MJ said waving his little hand.

"You want to hold him?" Zaria asked and MJ immediately began nodding his head yes. "Okay, get up here with me so you can hold him." She scooted over and patted the small, empty space beside her. MJ got ready to hop into the hospital bed until he was stopped by his grandmother.

"Wait one second, baby, give, me your coat." She told him, reaching to remove the black and blue North Face jacket that graced his back.

Once it was off, she let him proceed to hop up in the bed and get comfort next to his mother. Once he was good and situated, Zaria showed him how to position his arms before placing his baby brother into them. Walking over to the rocking chair that sat next to Zaria's bedside, Ms. Jefferson rested MJ's coat on the back of it, before taking a seat. Looking over at her grand boys, she gave a faint smile.

"If only Marcus were here to see this." She stated still staring at the baby.

Zaria's heart skipped a beat at the mention of his name. It was as if a cold chill came over her body, as flashes of her disloyalty began to go off inside of her brain. All she could think was, if Marcus were there to witness that moment, she would have most definitely been in the Intensive Care Unit instead of the maternity ward, and Gwahla would have been in a bed next to her; if not dead. One thing Marcus was big on was loyalty, and they had betrayed him in the dirtiest way possible.

Sighing deeply, Zaria tried to replenish the air that had left her body before she proceeded to reply. She wanted so badly to just come clean about everything she and Gwahla had done but she wasn't ready to suffer the consequences. She had two babies that depended on her and she'd be damned if she missed out on anything in their lives. They both would grow up without neither one of their parents, and she just couldn't let that happen. So, she did what she had been doing for the last few months; she played it cool.

"Yea, I wish he were here to witness this." Zaria smiled. "Our two, Prince's. Even though he wanted a little princess, I'm sure he would have been satisfied." She finished, staring at her boys with guilt.

"I'm sure." Ms. Jefferson replied dryly, glaring at nothing in particular.

Her soul was lost. Losing her baby boy had taken such a toll on her she didn't know whether she was coming or going. Certainly, she had some good days, but they only lasted a moment before reality sunk back in. She was numb without her son, and the possibility of the snakes that took him out being right in her front yard, didn't make the situation any better.

"I saw Gwahla on the way up." Ms. Jefferson gave a faint chuckle as she changed the subject.

Zaria's heart again skipped a beat; she could feel the back of her ears get hot as butterflies formed in the pit of her stomach; she was nervous as hell.

"Oh, d..did you?" She smiled still trying to play it cool, as she swallowed the dry lump in her throat. "Yea, he was just bringing me something to eat. You know this hospital food ain't the best." She slightly giggled, running her hand over her hair. Ms. Jefferson gave a faint smile.

"Oh, that was nice of him. He didn't tell me that, to my recollection he brought you in when you were in labor." She turned to look at Zaria just in time to notice the flush look, that'd suddenly graced her face. She knew that look all too well, she had been seeing it from she and Gwahla both, since her son's passing. It was the look of guilt.

"Oh, yea, yea! I really didn't have anyone else to call, so I called him." Zaria quickly answered.

"Oh, so I guess I'm nobody?" Ms. Jefferson shot back with a raised brow.

"No, no, that's not what I'm saying at all. I mean, it was late; I didn't want to bother you. You already had MJ, I didn't want you having to get out of your bed and lug him along too." Zaria continued to lie, digging her hole deeper and deeper.

"Oh, I see." Ms. Jefferson replied nonchalantly; again staring off at nothing in particular.

The room fell silent as neither one of the ladies said a word. Zaria didn't know what else to say; she was so nervous she could hear her own heart beating. Ms. Jefferson was acting really, unusual and Zaria had a feeling in her gut it was because she knew something. Usually Ms. Jefferson's presence was loving and warm, and she always kept a smile displayed on her face. This particular day she was cold as ice and bore a look that Zaria had never witnessed before; it was scary. The way she sat as stiff as stone in that rocking chair, staring into space, not saying a word, was freaking Zaria the hell out.

"Some detectives came by my house a few days ago," Ms. Jefferson blurted, breaking the awkward silence. "They told me that Terrence has all of a sudden changed his statement, would you happen to know anything about that, Zaria?" She asked.

The way she spun her head slowly in Zaria's direction, you would've thought she was some, kind of damn robot or special made clone. It was like she was being operated by someone. Zaria damn near shit bricks as Ms. Jefferson stared her dead in the eyes waiting for her reply. It was all, of a sudden getting hot, and it felt as if the walls were closing in on her. She knew it was only her anxiety, so she closed her eyes and took a deep breath before she replied.

"No, no, that's new news to me." Zaria blinked uncontrollably out of nervousness. "Why would he do that after all this time?" She then asked playing her role.

"Beats me." Ms. Jefferson shrugged. "I just thought maybe you would know since you two are so close." She finished. Zaria scoffed, letting out a small chuckle.

"Close? What makes you think we're close?" Zaria asked curiously.

"I mean, he's taking MJ to school in the mornings, making him pancakes in your kitchen, sleeping in your bed; not to mention, that damn baby doesn't look shit like a Jefferson!" Ms. Jefferson gave Zaria a smug look. "So cut the bullshit, little girl and spare me the lies. Something's going on, and you can either tell me or you can tell it to the police; your choice." Ms. Jefferson spat coldly. She was tired of the games, the lies, and pretending to be blind to the situation.

Zaria looked over at MJ's big mouth ass, who was too occupied with his new baby brother to even care what they were talking about. She knew that he was the only person that Ms. Jefferson could have gotten her information from and she was pissed. More so with herself than MJ though. He was just a kid and kids only spoke on what they saw. She only had herself to blame for exposing him to she and Gwahla's relationship in the first place. So, she couldn't fault her four, year old son for telling his grandmother about her dirty affair with her son's best friend.

Zaria didn't know what else to do, so she did what she knew how to do best. She put on her best performance and played victim.

"Marcus cheated on me first, he started all of this!" Zaria busted into tears. "He wasn't coming home, started getting real, disrespectful; he didn't give a damn about my feelings. I didn't mean for this to happen! It's just that Gwahla was there; he was my shoulder to cry on when Marcus left me home, all alone, to go fuck off with his new bitch!" She sobbed. Taking deep sniffles, she wiped the tears from her face with the palms of her hands.

"I fucked up, Ms. Jefferson and I regret it every day. I loved Marcus; things weren't supposed to be this way. Yes, Gwahla and I are closer than we're supposed to be, but you have, to believe me when I say I don't know nothing about him changing no statement or even speaking with the cops." She lied, still crying her eyes out.

Ms. Jefferson sat in silence as a tear slowly began to fall from her right, eye. She told herself every day that she'd wanted to know the truth about Zaria and Gwahla, when in all reality the truth was something she just couldn't handle; she was boiling on the inside. Out of all the shit her son had sacrificed for that trifling ass whore and that weak ass nigga, they had the audacity to betray him? Her heart just couldn't take it.

SLAP, SLAP!

Getting up from her seat, Ms. Jefferson abruptly gave Zaria two swift slaps to the face; one with the front of her hand across one cheek and a backhand against the other. Zaria's mouth hit the floor in disbelief as she held one side of her stinging face. Even though she felt she deserved to get the shit smacked out of her, Zaria couldn't believe Ms. Jefferson had the nerve to reach out and touch her ass. The sound effects from the slap was so loud that it'd alarmed MJ, causing his head to spring up like a Jack in a box.

"Get up, MJ, let's go!" Ms. Jefferson demanded, staring at Zaria with eyes filled with rage. If looks could kill, she would've definitely been D.O.A.

"But, Glammmmy!" MJ protested, glaring sadly from his grandmother, to his mother.

"NOW!" she seethed. "Give your mother that damn baby and come on!" she shouted meaning every word. MJ began to cry as his mother retrieved his baby brother from his little arms.

"Listen to grandma, okay." Zaria cried as she placed a kiss onto her son's forehead. "I love you, big boy." She then told him.

"But, I wanna stay with you and Mori." MJ cried.

"I know, I know but you can't right now. I promise to come and get you when we get out of here and you can spend all the time in the world with us."

"The hell you won't!" Ms. Jefferson intervened.

"What?!" Zaria's eyes quickly darted in her direction after that statement. "You can't just take my son away from me!" She spat. Ms. Jefferson scoffed.

"Chile, please! Who's gonna stop me?" She asked looking Zaria square in the eyes. "You better PRAY I don't find out you had something to do with my son's death, or you will NEVER see him again! You, trifling BITCH!" Ms. Jefferson was so upset spittle flew from her lips, as she quoted her last statement.

"Let's go, MJ!" She snatched her grandson's coat from the back of the rocking chair, followed by his wrist, before storming out of the hospital room, door.

Zaria sat back in the bed with Mori in her arms and began to cry her eyes out. Shit was definitely about to get real for her.

Chapter Seven

"Ahh shit, right there; just like that!" Brick moaned as he leaned up against the wall inside of a room, in the bando he and Shooter were trapping out of.

As on the regular, he was getting topped off by Tracy, one of the neighborhood dope fiends. It was something she did in exchange for her daily fix whenever she didn't have any money. All the homies from the block clowned his ass for letting a dope head suck on his dick, but Brick didn't give a fuck. Tracy was clean, fine and thick as fuck, she just liked to get high. Nevertheless, she had some fire ass brain.

"Damn girl, you got a nigga finna buss!" Brick bit down on his bottom lip as he shoved all, of his dick down her throat.

He had a hand full of her thick, wild, hair, thrusting his hips into the hole of her face, as if it were her pussy. Tracy gagged repeatedly as globs of spit seeped from her lips, leaking all over his wood as well as her blouse. She could barely breathe through her stuffed nostrils, but she refused to stop until Brick got his nut. All she could think about was the reward at the finish line; she could taste the crack smoke with every slurp.

"Aaarrrggghh, fuck! Sssssss!" Brick let out as he released himself into her warm, wet, mouth. As always, Tracey sucked him dry being sure to swallow every drop.

"Damn girl, I swear if you wasn't a rock head I'd marry you just for ya mouth alone!" Brick said chuckling as he pulled up his pants and fixed himself back up.

"Whatever, Brick. Just give me the shit, I gotta go!" Tracy said quickly wiping spit residue from her mouth and chin. She was jonesing so bad she could barely keep still.

"Damn, hold up." Brick chuckled. "Can a nigga put his dick up first?" He finished, fastening his Gucci belt followed by making sure his shirt was straight. He then reached into the pockets of his denim, True Religion jeans, and pulled out a twenty-dollar rock, handing it over to her. Tracy held the stone between her thumb and index tips, looking at it in disgust.

"Damn nigga, this it?" she scoffed.

"Fuck you mean?" Brick grimaced.

"I mean, I thought you was gon hook a sista up!" Tracy whined. "You had a bitch on her knees for damn near an hour, my jaws hurting and shit! You could at least give me a lil mo for the pain!" She finished as she rubbed the side of her face.

Brick huffed as he pulled another stone out of his pocket; this one only being ten-dollars, worth.

"Here, bitch! You better start bringing some money around this muthafucka, this shit ain't gon keep flyin." He seethed smacking the rock into the palm of her hand.

"Yea, yea, yea, that's what you said yesterday. See you later." Tracy snickered, quickly making her way out of the room. Brick shook his head in shame as he followed suit, making sure she left the trap. The last thing he needed was her ass sticking around trying to suck him dry for more rock.

Opening the front door of the bando, Brick let Tracy out. Happily skipping around the group of niggas shooting dice on the porch, she let herself out of the fenced in yard and disappeared up the block. Brick stepped onto the porch with his homies and took a seat in one of the, tan, fold up chairs.

"Let me bang that after you, Shooter." He stated referring to the blunt that was in rotation. The dice game instantly came to a halt and everyone looked in his direction.

"Ion know nigga. You bout been eating geeker pussy and

I don't want noooo parts of that!" One of the homies, TuTu, blurted causing everyone to fall out laughing. Brick instantly took offense.

"Nigga you got me fucked up, I ain't eating no geeker pussy! I just let the bitch suck my dick!" He seethed.

"Like that's any better." Another one of the homies chimed in as he proceeded to roll the dice.

"Right, and I bet the nigga didn't use a condom." TuTu shot back and everyone start laughing again.

"Aye, y'all get off my mans." Shooter said defending Brick as he passed him the gas.

"Right, my nigga. They act like they ain't never let a dope fiend bitch suck em off before, I know I ain't the only one. Besides, ain't shit wrong with it." Brick boasted taking a pull from the blunt.

"Now I ain't say all that shit, nigga. I don't give a fuck how hard life get, I ain't letting no fiend wax my shit." Shooter quickly let it be known. "I was just taking up for you because you my nigga and these niggas got you fucked up tryna embarrass you and shit." He finished. Pulling another freshly rolled blunt from behind his ear, he put it to his lips and fired it up.

"Man, ain't nobody tryna embarrass that weak ass nigga!" TuTu chuckled rolling the dice. "If he fuck geeks, he fuck geeks." He stated collecting his winnings from the seven he'd hit on the first shot.

"Aye, nigga, shut the fuck up. I'm bout sick of you!" Shooter grimaced in TuTu's direction.

"Nigga, what?!" TuTu shot back, snapping his neck in Shooter's direction.

"You heard what the fuck I said! Don't keep talking shit like I didn't see you ducking off in the alley with buck teeth Benetta's pipe smoking ass yesterday around 1:30." Shooter exposed his ass, expeditiously.

Everyone looked in TuTu's direction as they waited on his reply. Buck teeth Benetta was one of the dirtiest fiends from their hood. She had two big ass teeth in the front of her mouth, and it was obvious as fuck that she didn't brush them bitches. A flush of embarrassment came over TuTu as all eyes were on him. He wanted to deny Shooter's accusations so bad, but he couldn't, he had been spotted.

"Well," One of the homies stated letting TuTu know that they were waiting on his response.

"Now see, that was different!" He finally spoke up.

"Ahhhh, hell nah!" the whole porch said in unison before they all fell out laughing.

"I bet not ever catch you hitting my weed again nigga!" One of the homies immediately began clowning him. "You got the nerve to be talking about Brick and you getting face from Bugs Bunny's strung out ass lil sister?! Nigga you better go get yo rabies shot!" he finished.

"Aye, tell the truth, you was curious on how them two front teeth felt, huh nigga?" Brick added his two cents.

"Man, fuck y'all!" TuTu sucked his teeth in embarrassment.

They sat there driving his ass for a good little minute; they'd forgotten all about the dice game. Everyone was so busy talking their shit, they didn't even notice the black, Chevy Impala pulling in front of the trap. It wasn't until they heard the doors closing when they noticed the two detectives proceeding into their direction; all, of their smiles quickly left their faces.

"Who the fuck is this and what the fuck they want?" Shooter grimaced, watching the detectives as they made their way to the gate.

"Yo guess is as good as mine." Brick replied sucking his teeth, as he too watched closely.

"Gentlemen; how are you all this evening?" the Mexican one spoke up, greeting everyone on the stoop.

"Great, just minding our fuckin business. How can we help you?" Shooter got straight to the point. The last thing he needed was two detectives lingering around the spot, fucking up the money. Morales slightly chuckled.

"Well, I'm detective Morales and this is my partner detective Harrington." He introduced themselves. "We're looking for a couple of fellas by the names of Brian and Byron Myers; you all may know them as Fatz and Chubbz." He continued reading from his little note pad. "We were told they could be found in this..."

"Never heard of em." Shooter cut the Detective off before her could finish his statement.

"Come on man, don't bullshit us! We're working a serious murder case and it would be nice if you'd cut the crap." Morales seethed. He could smell the bullshit Shooter was trying to feed them from where he was standing, and they were a pretty good distance apart.

"And I told you I've never heard of em." Shooter made himself clear.

"Okay." Detective Morales nodded. "What about you boys?" He asked the rest of the guys on the porch.

"They ain't never heard of em neither." Shooter spoke up again.

"I think they can speak for themselves." Harrington intervened. The whole stoop of fellas began shaking their heads in unison.

"Nah, those names don't sound too familiar." Brick stated.

"They're not ringing any bells for me either, sir." TuTu added. Morales fell out laughing, hysterically.

"Oh, come on! You've got to be fucking kidding me, you bastards are fuck..."

Harrington quickly threw his hand up, halting the remainder of his partner's statement. He knew you could attract more bees with honey, so the last thing he wanted to do was piss off anyone who kept an ear to the streets. There was a way to do everything and Morales's way, surely wouldn't get them anywhere.

"Thank you for your time, fellas." Harrington stepped in. He then reached in the pocket of his suit jacket and pulled out one of his business cards. "If any one of you just so happen to get any information or bump into one of the Myer brothers, could you please give us a call?" He finished.

Harrington proceeded to reach for the latch on the gate but suddenly came to a halt.

"May I?" He asked before entering their fenced in property.

Shooter gave a slight head nod and Harrington stepped inside of the gate. Meeting Shooter halfway up the concrete steps, he extended his hand and gave him the card.

"Thanks, man. I appreciate your cooperation." Harrington said before turning to head back to their vehicle.

Shooter and his gang watched them all the way up until they were turning off, of the boulevard. When they were out of sight, he pulled out his phone and dialed up his big homie.

"Murder?! What the fuck they mean murder?" Brick asked as Shooter was placing the phone up to his ear.

"Fuck if I know. But I do know I'm about to put a bug in them nigga's ear." Shooter informed him.

"You ready to do this, bro?" Fatz asked as he looked over into the passenger seat at his little brother, Chubbz.

They were sitting outside of Teyanna's apartment getting ready to go in and pay Quincy's bitch ass a visit. It was something that Chubbz had been itching to do since he'd saved Teyanna from his severe beating.

"Nigga, what kind of question is that? I've been dyin to see this punk ass nigga." Chubbz replied as he slipped on a pair of black, leather gloves.

"Well, let's do this shit." Fatz told him cocking his black, Glock 40, placing it into the waistband of his jeans. "And remember, in and out! Ain't nobody got time for yo bullshit tonight." He finished, giving his brother a serious look.

Whenever they did their dirty work, Chubbz always wanted to prolong the process by torturing their victim. Especially the ones he had a personal hate for. Fatz on the other hand, didn't fuck around with the fuck around. He liked to do the job as quick as possible. In and out, was his motto.

"Nigga fuck you; don't tell me what to do! I do whatever I feel in that moment." Chubbz shot at his brother.

"Yea, iight. Do that shit tonight and watch me leave yo ass." Fatz replied.

"And? You act like I don't know how to rob a muthafucka for they shit to get me back where I need to be." Chubbz grimaced. Fatz instantly burst into laughter.

"Boy, you fucked up." He told him.

"What, you thought I was gon say I'd catch the bus or call a uber or some shit?" Chubbz smacked his teeth. "Nigga I'm a muthafuckin GANGSTA!" he finished, meaning every word.

"Well, nigga get yo gangsta ass the fuck up out this car so we can handle this business. I gotta get back up to the hospital to my bitch." Fatz stated.

"Yo ole soft ass!" Chubbz uttered as he proceeded to exit the vehicle.

Just as Fatz was about to follow suit, his cell began going off. Pulling it out of the pocket of his black, Levi jeans, he looked at the screen and noticed it was Shooter. Hitting the deny button, he quickly sent him to voicemail then placed his phone on silent. As he was doing that, his screen brightened, alerting him of a text; it was also from Shooter.

Get at me ASAP nigga...911

He read the text and his antennas immediately went up. He was about to return Shooter's call but just as he was about to click on the number, his little brother started running off at the mouth.

"Uhm, hello! Is we about to do this or is you about to sit there, texting love letters all fuckin night?!" Chubbz yelled through the passenger door.

"Man fuck you! Ain't nobody sending love text, bitch. This Shooter hitting me, 911." Fatz shot back.

"Man, fuck that nigga. He always hitting somebody up with 911's and don't be wanting shit!" Chubbz said with aggravation, as he quickly looked around the outside of the apartment complex for witnesses. "Man, hit that nigga back later. Ain't shit more important than what's about to go down. Let's do this shit and get the fuck up out of here before somebody see our ass!" He then told his big brother.

"Aiight, let's go." Fatz agreed without hesitation, tossing the phone into the cup holder and climbing out of the driver's seat. After all, Chubbz had a point, Shooter was known for hitting them up 911 when shit wasn't even an emergency. He was like the little boy who cried wolf; sending emergency messages for shit he could handle. Fatz just hoped like hell it wasn't really a fucking emergency.

Checking their surroundings once more, the brothers made their way towards Teyanna's doorstep; Chubbz leading the way. Upon arrival, he gave it a firm knock before covering the peephole with his left hand. After waiting for a few seconds and getting no response, he tapped a little bit harder. He wanted to bang on that muthafucka so bad, but he didn't want to draw any attention.

"What the fuck is taking this muthafucka so long?" Chubbz grimaced impatiently as they continued to wait for Quincy to come to the door.

"I don't know," Fatz sucked his teeth. "Maybe his ass ain't he…"

Before Fatz could finish his statement, they heard someone yell from the other side of the door. Chubbz quickly put his hand back over the peep hole, so whomever it was couldn't look out and see who was knocking.

"I said who the fuck is it!" They voice sounded closer, so they instantly knew the person had made it to the door.

Remaining quiet, Chubbz kept his hand over the hole, as Fatz screwed the silencer on his gun.

"Oh, I see what this is, somebody wanna get they ass whooped tonight!" The guy roared before they heard, the sounds of locks unlocking.

Fatz aimed his gun in the direction of the door as they waited for it to open. They didn't know if it was Quincy's hoe ass on the other side of the door but whomever it was, was about to catch a hot one to the dome as soon as they opened that bitch.

"A nigga tryna get his nut off and mufuckas knocking like they the damn po…" The door flung open and the nigga stopped in mid-sentence as he stared down the silencer of Fatz' gun.

"Man, what the fuck!" Chubbz turned up his nose as he looked the butt naked, man up and down in disgust. Instead of covering up his semi erect, genitals like any normal human being, he threw his hands up in surrender and commenced to pleading for his life.

"Please don't shoot me, I don't even live here!" He cried looking back and forth between the two brothers. Fatz looked him square in the eyes and let out a devilish chortle.

"Damn my nigga, that's unfortunate as fuck. But I gotta kill you just for answering the door with ya fuckin dick out! Where the fuck is your manners?!" Fatz seethed, biting fiercely into his bottom lip as he aimed his gun at the guy's head.

"Please, please, please," The guy begged over and over and he stood there with his eyes shut, tightly.

Before another *please* could escape the man's lips he saw black, but it wasn't from the back of his eyelids. Fatz had put a bullet in the nigga's head; right between his eyes. As his body slumped to the floor, blood began slowly seeping from his wound. Without looking down, Chubbz stepped over the nigga and invited himself into Teyanna's apartment to look for Quincy. Fatz followed suit after closing the front door behind them.

The living room area was empty, so the duo headed for the back of the apartment. As they got closer to the bedroom, they could hear sounds of a muffled voice. Chubbz pulled his gun from his waistband and immediately cocked it. When they made it to where the sound was coming from, the brothers were again disgusted with the sight before them.

"What the fuck kind of queer ass shit they got the fuck going on in here?!" Fatz asked with a dismantled facial expression, as his eyes landed on Quincy, whom was chained up to the bed on all fours, with a gag ball in his mouth. His skin was all sweaty and slippery looking, and he too was naked as the day he was born.

"Bruh, I don't even fuckin know, but I gotta get a picture to show my bitch." Chubbz laughed as he went into his pocket to retrieve his phone. Pulling it out he went to his camera and began snapping photos. "Nigga how the fuck you, beating on bitches and you in this muthafucka tooted up like one?" He continued laughing as he caught a shot from every angle.

"Man, aight that's enough, shit. Let's just kill this sick ass nigga and get the fuck up out of here. This shit making my stomach hurt." Fatz turned up his face, rubbing his belly in irritation.

"MMMAAA!?" Quincy muffled with buck eyes once Fatz made the reference to killing him. They could easily make out what he'd said, which was *WHAT.* Chubbz instantly fell out in laughter.

"What, nigga? You scared?" He asked as he tapped the barrel of his gun against Quincy's forehead. "We promised to make this as quick and painless as possible. Shit I planned on making you suffer; torture you a lil bit, but seeing the freaky ass shit you into. You, bout would've enjoyed what I had in mind." Chubbz finished, shaking his head in disgust.

Quincy immediately burst into tears. He didn't know why the hell Chubbz and Fatz were there or what they wanted; all he knew was he wasn't ready to die. One minute he was having the time of his life with one of his home boys, finger popping each other's assholes, and the next he was staring down the barrel of a gun. He closed his eyes praying it was all a dream, but when he opened them back up, the two brothers were still standing over him.

"Mmmm mm mmm, mmmmm!" Tears streamed down Quincy's face as he begged for his life through muffles.

Chubbz slapped his knee in laughter as he stared down at him, desperate and defenseless. The look of helplessness in his face made Chubbz' dick hard. Quincy was scared shitless and he loved every minute of it. The only thing he hated was Teynanna wasn't there to see it.

"Man, take this shit out yo fuckin mouth, we can't understand shit you sayin!" Fatz swiftly snatched the gag ball from the hole in his face. Just as soon as it was out, Quincy began running his mouth like a faucet.

"Please, please don't kill me! I'll do anything, man! I'll suck both ya'll dicks man, please!" He cried hysterically, hoping they'd take him up of his offer. Little did he know it didn't do shit but piss them off even more.

"Ew, what the fuck!" Fatz seethed, stuffing the ball back between Quincy's gay ass lips. "Man hurry up and shoot this sick ass muthafucka before I do!" Fatz finished, smacking his fruity ass over the head with the butt of his gun.

Quincy yelled out in agony as blood seeped from the corner of his right eyebrow. He then began muffling some more words, this time with a face filled with rage. Once again, neither of the brothers could make out what he was saying, so they took it as him talking his shit. It really didn't matter what the fuck he was saying, because before he could muffle another word, Chubbz let off three shots to his dome.

"Shut the fuck up, faggot!" He grimaced, firing one last shot into Quincy's ass.

Once solidifying that he was dead, the duo hopped into their vehicle and fled the apartment complex.

Whoop, whoop! Whoop!

Fatz and Chubbz made it a few miles away from Teyanna's place when they heard a sound that caused both of their hearts to, began racing. Looking into the review and side mirrors, they immediately started to panic as red and blue lights flashed behind them.

"What the fuck bro, I thought you said this whip was legit?!" Fatz uttered as he slowly veered to the shoulder of the road, pulling over. A small voice in his head was telling him to put the pedal to the metal and high speed their asses, but he didn't want to risk he and his brother's freedom doing some dumb shit.

"It is! Femo gave me registration and insurance papers." Chubbz replied, referring to the nigga he'd gotten the ride from as he popped the glove box open and began rambling. Pulling out the information, he flashed it to his brother.

"Iight, cool. We straight then. Just be cool and we'll be out of this lil jam in no time." Fatz stated as he continued staring out of his rearview mirror. "Here, put this in the spot." He then quickly passed his gun to Chubbz, being sure not to take his eyes off, of the squad car behind them.

Doing as he was told, Chubbz lifted the floor mat that rested beneath his feet and stashed their weapons in a hidden compartment. Locking it up, he placed the mat back in its proper place and sat back in his seat. Sighing deeply, they waited for an officer to approach their vehicle. The two of them damn near shit bricks when officers walked up on both sides. Swallowing hard, Fatz hit the button to let his window down.

"Good evening, officer." He put on a fake ass smile.

"Good evening, gentlemen. We stopped you because it seems you have a taillight out. Also, there's no light above your license plate so I couldn't read your tags." The African American officer, who appeared to be in his mid to late thirties, stated.

"Oh, I'm sorry about that, sir. I hadn't even noticed the light had gone out. Besides, this isn't my vehicle, it's one of my cousin's; they failed to mention it." Fatz replied, remaining calm as ever.

"It's alright, I just need your license and registration, and we'll have you guys out of here in no time." The officer told him.

Doing as he was asked, Fatz reached over to retrieve the registration papers from his brother and handed them over to the officer. He then held up his hand and motioned towards his left, pocket to inform the officer that he was about to reach for his wallet. After getting a head nod of approval, he grabbed his wallet and retrieved his identification. Handing it over to the officer, he threw the wallet into the cup holder.

"Alright, hang tight; I'll be right back." The officer assured him before heading back to his vehicle.

His partner remained planted at the passenger window and kept an eye on the duo. Chubbz remained silent, with his window still up and his face forward. He wasn't scared, he just wanted them to hurry the fuck up so he and his brother could be on their way; cops made him nervous and he didn't fuck with them on any type of level.

Fatz on the other hand wasn't worried at all. As long, as the paperwork to the vehicle they'd rented from his Mexican home-body earlier that day came back clean, they would be good to go. His name was clean besides the felony and a few misdemeanors he had on him, and as far as warrants, he didn't have any of those. He just hoped his brother was just as clean.

After about five, long minutes, Fatz finally noticed the officer making his way back to their car. He didn't notice any tickets in his hand, so he figured that was a good thing. The officer looked to have the same demeanor he had when he approached the car the first time, so that was a good thing as well. Fatz smiled on the inside as he made it back to their car and handed him back his information.

"Here you are, Mr. Myers. Your registration checked out and your insurance is good." The officer told him.

"Thank you, sir." Fatz smiled as he grabbed his license and registration.

"No problem, but I also need you and your passenger to please step out of the vehicles and place your hands behind your backs." The officer then demanded, shocking the fuck out of them both.

"Huh? I thought you just said we were good?" Fatz asked confused as to why they were being detained.

"No, I said your license, registration and insurance were good. You two, have a warrant for questioning." The officer informed them.

"Wait, warrant for questioning? Questioning for what?" Chubbz asked pissed, leaning over from the passenger seat.

"You guys will find that out once we make it to the station, I don't have an answer for that." The officer replied. "Now come on gentlemen, we don't have all night." He finished.

Fatz looked over at his litter brother and sighed deeply as Chubbz shook his head in disbelief. Doing as they were told they both exited the vehicle, placing their hands behind their backs. Even though they didn't know what they were being taking in to the station to be questioned about, they still cooperated. They didn't want to act a fool when it could have all be a misunderstanding in the end.

"What about or ride?" Fatz asked referring to their vehicle as he and his brother were being placed in cuffs.

"I'll be sure to lock it up for you. It's in a good spot, I'm sure no one will bother it." The officer placing on his cuffs assured him.

Once he was finished, he walked Fatz to the back of his car. Removing his keys from the ignition, Fatz watched the officer keep his word as he locked up their vehicle. Walking back over to him, he placed the keys into his right pocket before escorting him to the back of the squad car.

"Watch ya head, son." The officer stated as he opened the door and sat Fatz inside, behind the driver's seat.

Closing him in, he watched his partner place Chubbz in the back, passenger side, before they both got into the cruiser and headed for the station.

∞∞∞

You have reached the voicemail box of, **Fatz.** *After the tone, pl…*

"Uggh, where the fuck is this nigga at?!" Fragile huffed as she pressed the end button, hanging up the call and tossing the phone down onto the hospital bed. "I'm hungry and I'm tired of eating this damn hospital food!" She complained to Teyanna, who was in her room visiting, she and the baby.

They'd both made it an obligation to take turns visiting one another each day they'd been admitted into the hospital.

However, Teyanna would be discharged the next day and Fragile prayed that would be her fate also. She'd finally made a bowel movement like they wanted her to, and they were actually going to let her and the baby leave, but when they took her last set of vitals before discharging her, her blood pressure was sky high. After hours of not being able to get it down, they decided to keep her a little while longer. Well, it had been two days since then and Fragile was over it; she was ready to go.

"Girl, chill." Teyanna replied through snickers. "You sound spoiled as hell. He may be busy doing something, just give the man some time." She finished.

"What could he possibly be doing that requires his phone being off? If you ask me, the only time a person powers their phone off is when they doing some shit they ain't got no business." Fragile smacked her lips. "You know what; matter of fact, call Chubbz." Fragile then demanded.

"Oh my God, you so extra!" Teyanna huffed, rolling her eyes to the top of her head as she pulled her phone from the pocket of her hospital gown. "What, I ain't keeping you enough company?" She asked, scrolling through her call log.

"Bitch bye, it ain't even like that!" Fragile scoffed. "I just miss my teddy bear!" She oozed, blushing from ear to ear.

"Oooh, now he ya teddy bear? Just a few months ago, he was a fat fuck with titties!" Teyanna laughed as she hit Chubbz' contact and placed the phone up to her ear.

"You know what? Fuck you, okay!" Fragile couldn't do shit but laugh as she flipped her friend the bird. The two shared a moment of laughter as Fragile watched Teyanna call Chubbz, waiting for him to pick up.

"That's weird, his phone goin straight to voicemail, too." Teyanna stated with a screw face, as she pulled the phone from her ear and looked at it. Hitting his name again she called once more, only to get the same result.

"Bitch, I don't know now. I'm starting to feel like you, where the fuck these niggas at?" Teyanna stated hitting the end button before slipping the phone back into her gown.

"See, but I'm trippin." Fragile smacked her lips. "It ain't even been six months and they already on fuck shit! I ain't got time for this shit, this nigga got me fucked up; I'm bout to text his ass. I bet you he call after this." She finished picking her phone back up, getting ready to text Fatz a piece of her mind. She was in the middle of a sentence when Teyanna snatched the phone from her fingers.

"Bitch, what the fuck is you doin? Give me my phone back!" Fragile spat, looking at Teyanna as if he were crazy.

"Nah, I'm stopping you before you text something stupid." Teyanna shot back, deleting the sentence Fragile had started. "Clearly you haven't dealt with a REAL, hood nigga so you don't know how to handle one. Instead of texting some dumb shit thinking it's going to make him reply, you need to be making sure the man is okay!" Teyanna schooled her best friend. "Hell, they could be somewhere dead and here you go texting his phone with crazy shit!" She finished, handing Fragile her phone back.

"Damn, you right, huh?" Fragile took a minute to think about what her friend was saying. "Bitch I'm just all fucked up. Ever since finding out Marcus had a whole family right up under my nose and I didn't know shit, makes me not put shit past no nigga. They all sneaky as fuck if you ask me."

"Nah, you can't be like that, friend." Teyanna disagreed, shaking her head. "What has Fatz done to show you that he's just like all the rest of these niggas? Because if you ask me, he ain't been shit but trill since day one. What nigga you know step in and take care of another nigga's responsibilities? Dead or deadbeat, I don't know not one!" Teyanna laughed. "Nah, but for real, he adores you and that baby, friend. Don't run him away." She finished.

After giving her friend's advice a quick thought, Fragile sighed deeply. As much as she hated to admit it, she was preaching to the choir.

"Uggggh, why do you always have to be so right?! You get on my damn nerves!" Fragile chuckled.

"Yea, whatever. Bitch you happy you have me for a best friend." Teyanna shot back.

"Shit, you ain't told no lies. I don't know what the hell I'd do without you."

"Awwww, I love you too bitch!"

Knock, knock!

Interrupting their little girl chat, was a knock at the door.

"Come in." Fragile sang, and in walked a bubbly, blonde, blue eyed nurse.

"Hi, mom. How are you guys doing." She stated, waving at Fragile then Teyanna. Teyanna politely waved back.

"Hii, we're pretty good for the most part." Fragile smiled, looking over inside of the cubby at a sleeping baby Emerald.

"Awwww, look at the little sleeping beauty; she's so gorgeous!" The nurse complimented taking, a peek.

"Thank you." Fragile snickered.

"Well, I have good news. You two get to go home tomorrow!" The nurse stated, silently clapping.

"Yessss!" Fragile gloated.

"I know, right? I know you're a happy camper; it's been a while."

"Yes, too long! I miss my bed, this one sucks." Fragile giggled along with the nurse.

"I bet. Just one more night and you're free as a bird!" The nurse replied. "Well, I only came to check up on you guys and give you the good news; I'll leave you guys be. Would you like for me to take her or do you want to keep her here with you?" she then offered, referring to baby Emerald.

"As much as I hate to do it, ima let you take her! Since this is my last night, I want to get some rest; this might be the last time I get a full night's rest for a while." Fragile replied, rolling her eyes to the top of her head.

"You got that right." The nurse slightly chuckled. "Well, I will grab her and be on my way. If I don't get to see you before you leave, congratulations again and I wish you the best on your motherhood journey!" she finished, grabbing the edge of baby Emerald's cubby and rolling it towards the door.

"Thank you!" Fragile smiled.

"You guys have a good night!"

"You too!" Fragile and Teyanna replied in unison as they watched her exit the room with the baby. When she was gone, the ladies continued chatting.

"Thank God I get to finally go hooooome!" Fragile sang doing the happy dance from her hospital bed. "Now I just gotta find out where this nigga is so he can make sure he's here to get us." She finished.

"I know right, and this nigga still ain't responded to my text message; I hope everything's okay." Teynana added, checking the screen on her phone.

"Shit, me too. Let me text Fatz." Fragile picked up her phone back up. Going to her messages, she went to his name and began typing.

Call me as soon as you get this message babe, we're being released tomorrow. -Fragile

She then hit send and took a deep breath.

"Hopefully he hits back soon; I'm starting to get worried. This isn't like either of them." She told Teyanna.

The whole time they'd been kicking it with the two brothers, there was never a time where they couldn't get ahold of them. This was the first and shit just didn't seem right. They might not have known them like the back of their hands just yet, but they knew them well enough to know that they didn't turn their phones off; ever.

"They will, friend. My gut feeling is telling me they will." Teyanna replied, but on the inside, she was just as worried.

∞∞∞

"So, how do you suggest we do this? You wanna do good cop bad cop, bad cop bad cop, or..."

"I don't think we should do any of that." Harrington held up his hand, cutting his partner off in mid-sentence. "I just think we should go in, ask what we want to know and see what they tell us. We can't come off too aggressive; guys like them be waiting on us to come off too strong so that they can lawyer up. Let's just be cool and try to get as much information as possible." He finished. Grabbing his file from the desk they were standing at he led the way towards the interrogation rooms.

"Okay, okay, cool it is. I'll let you run the show." Morales replied in tow.

"Thank you." Harrington turned and smiled in mid stride.

Once making it to interrogation room 1, he invited himself and his partner in without warning. Closing the door behind them, he tossed the manila folder that occupied his hand onto the rectangular shaped table and introduced himself.

"Good evening Mr. Brian Myers. I am detective Harrington, and this is my partner Morales; how are you tonight?" Harrington asked, extending his hand for a shake. Fatz stood and shook his hand then Morales's, before retaking his seats. Morales and Harrington took seats across the table from him.

"I was fine until I got brought up in here." Fatz replied leaning back in his chair, folding his arms across his chest.

"Yea, that's understandable. Well, we'll get straight to it then and hopefully we can get you out of here soon." Harrington told him.

"Yea, aight." Fatz sucked the gold on his teeth.

"Alright, my man." Harrington uttered as he opened his file and took, a peek. "So, can you tell me what you did from the time you got up to the time you went to bed on July 27th." He then asked, closing the folder back up.

Fatz nearly shit bricks. Hearing the date that left the detectives mouth was a dead giveaway as to why he was there. He would never forget it; that night would forever be burned in his brain. It was the night that he, his brother and cousin, gunned down what turned out to be his girlfriend's, baby's father. The night he'd shredded her heart into pieces. The night he regretted ever happened. Yet, he played like he knew nothing.

"July 27th?" Fatz gave a slight chuckle. "that was like what, over three months ago? I can barely remember what I did three days ago. No disrespect sir, but do you know how many blunts I smoke?" he asked, rhetorically. Detective Harrington chortled lightly.

"Nah, man, I can only imagine. But listen, for your sake, I'm going to need you to think long and hard so that you can remember." Harrington told him straight up.

Fatz sighed deeply as he began fondling the hair that graced his chin. Thinking back on the day in question, he began to tell the detectives what he remembered.

"Aight so, if I can recall, I woke up around 9 AM. Got out the bed, rolled me up one, made me some coffee; cause see I can't take my morning shit without coffee and a blunt." Fatz mentioned before proceeding. "So, after I made my coffee, light cream and extra sugar, because I hate when my coff... "

"MR. MYERS!" Morales shouted frustrated, scaring the shit out of Fatz and his partner; causing them to slightly flinch.

"Damn, what's up?" Fatz asked nonchalantly. "Calm down, why you gotta yell and shit?" he asked, with a look as if he were really concerned. "You should be more like your partner; see, look how humble he is." Fatz pointed out, being a sarcastic ass-hole.

"Mr. Myers, carry on; and please leave out the unnecessary details." Harrington asked calmly but seriously. Fatz could see the solemnity in his facial expression, so he decided to cut the horse play. He also noticed how Morales was biting the insides of his jaws, so he knew he was a little tight as well.

"Aight, ima be real." Fatz sat up, resting his elbows on top of the table. "On July 27th, I was with family. It was our family re-union weekend; we kicked it from sunup to sundown." Fatz stated honestly.

"Okay," detective Harrington stated as he picked up his pen and began jotting down notes. "and is there anyone that can attest to that alibi?" he asked.

"I mean, ya'll got my little brother in the next room, ya'll can ask him." Fatz replied.

"Anyone else besides your brother?"

"Yea, my mother!" Fatz grimaced staring him dead in the eyes.

"Okay, and you never left your family?" Harrington threw another question.

"Nah, I didn't." Fatz started back fondling with his beard. "Aye, ya'll wanna tell me what this shit about?" He then asked, looking from Morales back to Harrington. Harrington sat his pen down and got straight to the point.

"We're working the homicide of Marcus Jefferson; you may have known him by his street name, Chief." He sat up staring Fatz right in the face, so that he could read every expression he was giving. Little did he know, Fatz was a blank book.

"Chief? Nah, that name doesn't ring a bell."

"Hmp," Harrington ran his hand over his salt and pepper, goatee. "that's funny, because we have a witness who's saying they saw you and your brother, hanging out the window of an all, black SUV, gunning down Mr. Jefferson in front of St. Louis Nights, nightclub a little after 3 AM."

"Bullshit!" Fatz protested. "Ain't nobody, see me hanging out of shit, doing shit, because I wasn't there." He finished.

"And your brother?" Morales chimed in.

"What about him?" Fatz grimaced, looking over at him.

"Where was he? You said YOU weren't there, so was he?" Morales asked.

"I just told ya'll we were with family. What part of that don't you understand? He... was... with... me...!" Fatz stressed, looking them both square in the eyes. "I don't know no Marcus, Chief, none of that." He finished, sucking his teeth.

"Okay, okay, we get it." Harrington nodded, motioning his hand as if he were telling Fatz to cool down. "Those names don't ring a bell, but what about the name Fragile Banks?" He then asked.

Fatz Antennas rose at the mention of Fragile's name. What did she have to do with anything? Yeah, she was Cheif's girl at the time of his murder, but how'd they figure she had any affiliations with him? He began to wonder if she'd put two and two together and found out who he and his brother really were. The thought quickly left his head just as soon as he remembered what the detective had said. He said they had a witness; meaning the person either saw, or knew what was going down, so he knew it couldn't have been her. He clearly remembered Fragile telling him that she didn't know or see anything. Either way, the detectives knew something, so he needed to be real, careful with his statements.

"Yea, I know her; that's my girl." Fatz replied honestly. "But what she got to do with this?" he then asked.

"So, you know she was the girlfriend of Mr. Jefferson at the time he was murdered? To my understanding she was with him; witnessed him take his last breath." Harrington threw out there.

"Nah, I didn't know that, but I know now." Fatz sucked his teeth, remaining undisturbed.

"So, you mean to tell me that you're seeing a girl, whom just lost her child's father a little over three months ago, and you don't know ANYTHING about it?" Harrington challenged.

"I didn't say that."

"So, what are you saying, Mr. Myers?" Morales questioned curiously.

"I knew she'd lost her child's father; I just never knew who he was. She never elaborated on that. She doesn't really like to talk about it, so I don't make her. I'm just there to make sure her and the baby is good. I know it's hard for her raising her daughter without a father, so I help her out anyway I can." Fatz explained.

"So, how did you two, meet?" Harrington then asked.

"I met Fragile at Family Dollar about a month after her baby father was killed; she was the cashier who rang me out. I thought she was beautiful as fuck so, I had to shoot my shot." Fatz shrugged with a chuckle. "She turned me down, highlighting the fact that she was pregnant and told me to go the fuck about my business, and I did." He continued smiling as if he was reminiscing on that very day. "A few days later, I saw her and her friend standing at the bus stop in the pouring rain. So, me and my brother stopped and gave them a ride."

"And they just got right in?" Harrington asked as if the story he was telling was bullshit.

"I mean, nah, they didn't get right in. It took some time, but eventually she took me up on my offer."

"Oh, okay. So, what happened after that?" Harrington wanted to hear more. He still wasn't convinced if he was being truthful or not.

"On the ride to her crib, I asked her what kind of nigga let's his baby mother catch the bus in the rain, she got super offended. That's when I found out that he was killed a month prior. I saw it was a sensitive subject, so I left well enough alone. From that day forward, we've just been real good friends. We really don't have a title; we both just know what it is." Fatz finished, hoping he'd told them everything they wanted to know; he was ready to get the fuck up out of there.

"So, if we go in there and ask your brother everything, we asked you the stories with be the same?" Morales asked.

"Why don't ya'll just go in there and see." Fatz replied sitting back in his seat, folding his arms back across his chest; he was done talking. From that moment, they were going to have to take the little information he did give and do what they got paid to do; investigate.

"Alight, hang tight. We'll be right back." Harrington stated getting up from his seat.

Gathering his file and notes, he and Morales headed across the hall to interrogation room 2. Once asking Chubbz the same questions and getting the same answers they'd gotten from his brother, they had no choice but to let them go. Escorting them to the parking lot of the station, they gave them a courtesy ride back to their vehicle.

"Thanks for your cooperation, gentlemen. Sorry to take up so much of your time." Harrington stated as he hit the lock on the doors, letting them out at their destination.

"No problem, we hope you solve your case and get who you're looking for. Shit wicked out here." Fatz said getting out of the back of their Impala, closing the door behind him. Chubbz on the other hand didn't say shit, he just got out and headed straight for their ride; he was still pissed.

"You fellas take care." Morales gave a slight smile and waved. They watched as the brothers got into their vehicle and started their engine, before pulling off.

"So, what do you think?" Harrington then asked, looking over into the passenger seat at his partner.

"You're not going to believe this, but I believe them." Morales replied. Harrington instantly let out a laugh.

"Well look at God!" He then stated.

"Oh, fuck you!" Morales joined in on the laughter.

"I'm just saying, that's unusual. You sure you're not coming down with something?" Harrington reached over and felt on Morales's forehead. Morales quickly smacked his hand away.

"No, but seriously." He cut the laughter. "The more we talk to people the more I'm starting to believe that Mr. Gwahla is the man behind all of this. Once we get a chance to get Fragile's side, we'll be able to put all of this shit together." Morales sighed.

"Well, we'll check and see if she's still in the hospital first thing in the morning. If she isn't, we'll go pay her a visit." Harrington replied. Morales didn't say anything back, he just gave a head nod still deep in his thoughts.

Harrington smiled on the inside as he continued back to the station. This was the first time in a long time, he'd witnessed Morales take one of their cases serious and he was proud. He figured their little exchange of words must have gotten to him; he just hoped that it stuck. Maybe they would be able to solve Marcus Jefferson's case together after all.

Chapter Eight

"You mind telling me just what the, FUCK that was?!" Chubbz snapped as soon as they walked into their spot, slamming the door behind him.

"Bruh, chill, damn! We free ain't we?" Fatz replied tossing the keys onto the table.

"Fuck that! How the fuck we getting questioned for some shit that went down MONTHS ago?! There was NOTHING to trace back to us, so I'm fuckin lost! And when was you gonna tell me that Fragile was the nigga's bitch? Fuck kinda shit you got going on, bruh?" Chubbz seethed, pacing the living room floor.

"Bruh, I said chill. It's not what the fuck you think!"

"Apparently it is, nigga! We almost just got fuckin BOOKED!"

"Noooo, we just got questioned. Now if you sit the fuck down and let me explain this shit, you'll know what the fuck is up!" Fatz barked, sucking his teeth.

Taking a seat on the sofa, he grabbed a sack of weed from underneath the sofa cushion to the left of him and proceeded to roll a fat ass blunt. Chubb took a squat on the loveseat across from him. Granted he was pissed, he still felt obligated to hear his big brother out. He had never been a fuck up in the past, so he knew it had to be a good explanation behind it all.

"Aight, so what's up?" Chubbz stated, letting Fatz know that he was all ears.

"I fucked up. I should've told you this shit when it happened, but I didn't think nothing was going to happen behind it." Fatz huffed shaking his head in shame as he sealed the blunt up. Grabbing a lighter from his pocket, he proceeded to dry it.

"Bruh, what the fuck you do?!" Chubbz automatically assumed the worst.

"The night Fragile's water broke, we had stopped at Walmart before the shit happened. We was just on some fuck off shit, getting lil items for baby girl." Fatz began, firing up the blunt and taking a long puff. "Anyway, while we were there, we ran into that nigga Gwahla. All, of a sudden, baby took off on the nigga and some pregnant bitch he was with; recording them with her phone and everything. The whole time I'm wondering how the fuck she know the nigga." He took another puff from the blunt before passing it over to his brother. Chubbz snatched the blunt from his grasp and quickly placed it up to his lips. He didn't like how the story was going, nevertheless he continued to listen.

"So, he reached for Fragile's phone trying to snatch it from her, and that's when I made my presence known; scary ass nigga looked as if he'd saw a ghost. Next thing I know, the bitch with him started faking like she was in labor and shit, drawing attention to us. I knew the bitch was faking because she was fine until shit started goin left between Gwahla and Fragile. The store clerk came over and started asking for EMT over her radio and shit; I grabbed Fragile's hand and we got the fuck up out of there. When we made it to the crib and I asked her how she knew the nigga, she told me that he was her baby daddy's best friend and that the bitch he was with was his other baby mama. That's when I put the shit together; I asked if Chief was her baby's father and she confirmed that he was. I instantly began feeling like shit." Fatz shook his head, running everything down to his brother.

Chubbz sat there as stiff as a board; he couldn't believe what he was hearing.

"So, you tryna tell me, all this shit is a big ass coincidence?" he then asked, passing the blunt back to his brother.

"The shit fucked me up too, bruh." Fatz replied taking another pull from the dope.

"Nah, I don't believe it." Chubbz shook his head. "How you don't know this bitch ain't been playing you all this time? She knows who the fuck we are, can't you see that! It's only a matter of time before we go down for fuckin murder!" Chubbz slammed his right fist into the palm of his left hand.

"Nah, bruh!" Fatz quickly shook his head. "She don't know shit, trust me bro. She was in that car the night we gunned the nigga down. If she knew it was us, she would've been turned our asses in. She hurt as fuck behind this shit. She honestly feels Gwahla is behind this shit, which is true. But I gotta tell her the truth."

"What?! Nah, fuck nah! Why the fuck would you do that?" Chubbz seethed, looking at his brother like he'd lost his mind.

"Because bro, the detectives are going to go see her next, you know how this shit go! If she finds out that we killed him and didn't hear it from me, she's going to assume this was all a set up. Versus if I come clean and tell the truth, we can possibly get her on our side and all this shit will fall back on Gwalah." Fatz finished.

"Man, are you dumb?! She gonna nail all of our asses to the cross!" Chubbz shot back.

"I mean bruh, what other choices do we have? It ain't like we had beef with the nigga, Gwahla paid us to do that shit! When she finds that out, she ain't gonna be tripping off us." Fatz stated hoping he was right. He didn't even believe the shit he was saying, but what other choices did they have.

Chubbz sat there for a minute and gave it some thought as he took long pulls from the blunt. The more he pondered the more he felt his brother was probably right. It was either take their chances and try to her Fragile on their side, or possibly end up going to jail for murder. He didn't like the thought of either, but they had way too much to lose to sit around and wait for the outcome. Blowing heavily, Chubbz blew out a huge cloud of smoke.

"What the fuck you waiting on? Get yo ass up and get dressed so we can get back up to this fuckin hospital!" he then told Fatz, getting up from the loveseat.

"My muthafuckin nigga!" Fatz smirked, getting up from the sofa.

"Nigga fuck you! I'm still pissed, but I'll never turn my back on you. We in this shit together." Chubbz told him.

"Fasho, from the cradle to the grave, nigga." Fatz replied as the two slapped fives and shared an embrace.

"From the cradled to the grave." Chubbz replied, before they parted ways to go freshen up for the day.

∞∞∞

Ms. Jefferson pulled up to Café ` Osage and parked her candy red, 2018 Genesis. Shutting off the engine, she grabbed her black, leather Michael Kors bag from the passenger seat and got out. Pointing her keypad towards her car, she locked it up as she made her way into the restaurant. Once inside, she scanned the place for the person she was meeting. Noticing them waving their hand in the air, she strutted in their direction.

"Margaret Banks?" She asked as she approached the woman she was meeting, being sure she was at the right table.

"That will be me!" Nana Banks smiled, standing to greet her.

"It's so nice to meet you." Ms. Jefferson returned the smile, giving her a firm handshake.

"Same here; I'm happy you could make it." Nana replied. "Here, have a seat; I was waiting on you to arrive before I ordered anything." She told her.

"Oh, girl, you didn't have to do that." Ms. Jefferson told her as she took a seat. After getting situated, she picked up the menu.

"I've actually never been to this place, are they new?" She asked as she looked over what they had to offer.

"No, they've been here quite a while. It's actually one of my favorite spots. Their egg benedict is to die for!" Nana Banks bragged.

"Oh, really? I guess I'm going to have to try that."

"Yes, I promise you won't be disappointed." Nana Banks assured her.

"Okay, well egg benedict it is!" Ms. Jefferson closed her menu and place it back in its original place.

Holding her hand up, she then called for a waiter. When they approached, she ordered the egg benedict, per Nana Banks request, with a mimosa. Nana Banks ordered the same, only she had plain orange juice, instead of it being spiked with champagne. It was a little too early for her to have any type of alcohol; she'd mess around and be sleep by noon.

"So, I know you're probably wondering why I found you on Facebook and asked for you to meet me." Nana Banks got straight to the point, just as soon as the waiter left to put in their orders.

"Girl, I didn't know who you were. I was like who is this messaging me with Michelle Obama as their profile picture? I almost didn't open it." Ms. Jefferson stated with a light chuckle. "But once I read the message, I had to give you a call."

"I know, and I apologize for that. I'd only made the page to find you; I don't do the social media thing, so I didn't want anyone to know I had a page." Nana explained.

"Oh well, that's understandable." Ms. Jefferson shrugged.

"Well," Nana Banks cleared her throat as she prepared for what she was about to say.

She had been waiting for the opportunity to share the news with Ms. Jefferson about her new grandbaby, but now that she was face to face with her, it was as if she couldn't find the words. Her heart was racing, and her palms were sweaty, and Ms. Jefferson sitting there staring her dead in the face, waiting on her next statement wasn't making it any better. Sighing deeply, Nana Banks swallowed her pride and proceeded.

"As you know, Fragile is my granddaughter." She stated and Ms. Jefferson gave a head nod letting her know that she was well, aware. "She and your son were dating before his passing. Well, a few weeks after his funeral she found out she was pregnant. I'm here because she gave birth to the baby a couple of weeks ago and I felt it was only right for you to know that you have a granddaughter." Nana Banks informed her.

Reaching into her pocketbook, she pulled out her phone. Going straight to her photo gallery she pulled up a picture of baby Emerald and handed it over to her.

"Her name is Emerald Jewel Banks." Nana Banks then told her.

Ms. Jefferson sat there speechless as she stared at the picture. Her heart suddenly felt full, and a sense of peace ran through her body. It was as if she were looking at her son all over again. Everything about baby Emerald was so perfect and just by looking at her, she could tell she was definitely one of theirs.

Gently running her finger over the screen, a few tears began to escape her eyes. Her son had always wanted a baby girl, and she wished so bad that he were there to share that moment with her. What she wouldn't do to have her baby boy back.

"I always knew it was more between those two." Ms. Jefferson sniffled, drying her bottom, eyelids. "He would always try to downplay their relationship, thinking I would judge him because he had his child's mother at home, but I knew what was going on; a mother always knows." She was talking to Nana Banks but was still staring at baby Emerald's photo.

"He didn't love that girl; he was only holding on because he didn't want to lose his son. He was in love with your grandbaby."

Ms. Jefferson tried so hard to fight back the tears, but they suddenly came pouring down.

Quickly snatching a few napkins from the napkin holder that graced the table, Nana Banks handed them over to her. Her heart went out to Ms. Jefferson; she couldn't imagine losing her child. As much as she couldn't stand her no, good daughter, Diamond, she still loved her dearly, and would lose her mind if she'd ever gotten that call.

"That's exactly why I reached out to you. I knew Marcus well; he was an absolute gentleman. And if I don't know nothing, I know he loved Fragile dearly. But ever since the day of his funeral, she has it in her mind that everything he ever told her was all a lie. He kept her in the dark about his child and his child's mother; she never knew about them. So, when she did find out, it was as if she really, never knew him. She didn't want to tell you about Emerald, but I begged to differ. You have the right to be in your grand daughter's life despite whatever she feels about her father." Ms. Jefferson told her.

"Thank you!" Ms. Jefferson stated. "God truly works in mysterious ways. I was going to search for Fragile but instead, he brought her to me. I guess with everything that's been going on, he knew I needed some help." She slightly chucked to keep from shedding another tear.

Briefly interrupting their conversation, the waiter came back to the table with their drinks. Which was right on time because Ms. Jefferson definitely, could use her mimosa. When the waiter left, they continued their discussion.

"So, if you don't mind me asking, what were you going to search for Fragile for?" Nana Banks questioned before taking a sip of her orange juice.

"Well, you may not believe me when I tell you this, because I was totally blown by it, but about a month after Marcus's funeral, his lawyer stopped by to leave me his will and a few other important documents. Lo and behold EVERYTHING he'd owned, including his personal bank accounts, he left to Fragile Banks." Ms. Jefferson revealed, causing Nana's bottom jaw to hit the floor.

"Oh, my Lord!" she whispered in disbelief, cupping her hand over her mouth.

"Oh, my Lord is right; Fragile and Emerald are set for LIFE and she doesn't even know it. He even left the store that he'd purchased for Zaria, in her name." Ms. Jefferson added.

Nana Banks sat there speechless. All this time her grandbaby had been going around believing everything that she and Marcus had shared was all a lie, meanwhile the whole time he was securing her future. If Fragile knew that, she would be devastated. Nevertheless, she was a very wealthy woman.

"Are you okay, did I say something wrong?" Ms. Jefferson asked, snapping Nana out of her thoughts. Nana Banks gave a slight chuckle; she hadn't even noticed she'd zoned completely out.

"Oh, no, you're fine." She replied picking up her juice, taking a quick sip. "It's just that I thought I would be dropping a bomb on you with the news about baby Emerald and you just dropped one on me." Nana told her.

"Well, I guess we're even." Ms. Jefferson shrugged and let out a small chortle.

"I guess so, huh?" Nana shot back.

She didn't know how she was going to tell Fragile about her little meeting with Ms. Jefferson after she'd clearly expressed that she wanted nothing to do with Marcus's family. On the other hand, she really didn't care. She was the grandparent and Fragile needed to know she was making a big mistake. She just hoped she wouldn't be too upset.

"So, on a lighter note, when do I get to meet my grandbaby?!" Ms. Jefferson gushed, placing a big, bright smile on her face.

She and Nana Banks had a wonderful brunch, laughing, talking and getting to know one another. They set up a date for her to come over to Nana's home to speak with Fragile and meet baby Emerald. Ms. Jefferson just prayed that Fragile would hear her out and welcome her into their lives.

∞∞∞∞

"Hey pretty girl! Hey mommy's pretty girl! We get to go home, yes we do!"

Fragile cooed at baby Emerald as she got her dressed. They were about to be discharged and she couldn't have been more, happy. She missed her home, her comfortable ass bed and her jacuzzi bathtub. Not to mention the homework she had to catch up on. Even though Nana worked her last nerve, she couldn't deny that she missed her worrisome ass too.

She had to admit though, being in the hospital gave her a lot of time to think and reevaluate her life. Having baby Emerald had given her a new sense of drive and motivation. All she could think about was finishing school so that she could obtain her nursing degree. Being that she was the only parent baby Emerald had, there was no time for slacking. Granted she had Fatz, but who was to say he would be around forever? It was time to get on her grown woman and rise, up.

Knock, knock.

Fragile heard light taps on the door, followed by the door opening and someone walking in. She didn't even get a chance to tell them that they could enter. Thank God she'd already gotten herself dressed and was only tending to baby Emerald. She would've been pissed if she were caught unpleasant.

As soon as the person appeared out of the doorway and into the room where she could see, Fragile smacked her lips and rolled her eyes to the top of her head. It was Fatz' big, sexy ass bearing flowers and a teddy bear, with a big ass smile on his face.

She didn't know why the hell he was grinning so damn hard; she surely hoped he didn't think those flowers and that cheesy ass bear would make her forgive him for having her up all fucking night, worried half to death. It only made her want to punch his ass dead in his ugly face.

"What's up, beautiful." He asked, walking over and placing a kiss onto her cheek. Fragile didn't budge, she just continued dressing baby Emerald.

"Damn, so it's like that?" Fatz chuckled licking his lips. She could tell that he was higher than Snoop Dog, in a hot air balloon. That alone made her assume that he'd been out up to no good. Therefore, she had no words for his ass.

"So, you just gon give a nigga the silent treatment?" he asked, and still got no reply.

Fatz instantly began to worry. Fragile hadn't ever given him the silent treatment and the only thing he could think, was that the detectives had been by to pay her a visit. She bore a smug look on her face that let him know that she was indeed pissed at him. He wanted so badly to turn around and walk right back out the door, but instead he stayed to check and see just how high her temperature was.

Placing the bouquet of roses down onto the hospital table, along with the stuffed bear, Fatz took a seat in the rocking chair that rested directly next to the bed.

"Y'all all dressed up and shit, y'all going somewhere?" He asked still trying to get Fragile to talk to him. Scoffing, she cut her eyes at him.

"If you would've had your phone on last night, you would know the answer to that question." She then spat, placing a pair of pink booties onto baby Emerald's little feet. Fatz smacked his teeth.

"So, that's what you mad about?" He asked with a screw face. "Man, chill. "You don't even know the reason my phone was off;

shit, I almost didn't even make it back to this muthafucka." He finished.

"What you mean?" Fragile asked.

"Just what I said. We damn near went to jail last night." He informed her, causing her attitude to shift.

"Oh my God, why? What happened?" She asked more concerned than angry.

"We got pulled over and they took us in for questioning on some shit that went down a while back. Look, I gotta talk to you but I don't wanna do it here." He stated honestly.

"Okay, cool. We're about to get discharged; I was just waiting on Nana to get here. But since you're already here, I can just call and tell her not to come. She was busy doing something anyway." Fragile shrugged.

"Aight, cool." Fatz replied as he stared off into space, thinking of how he was going to break the news to her.

Grabbing her phone, Fragile dialed up Nana Banks to inform her that she no longer needed to make the trip to the hospital, because Brian would bring them home. To her surprise she didn't make a stink about it; she simply agreed and told her that she would see them whenever they made it to the house. Which was unusual because she always had something to say. Especially when had anything to do with Brian.

Ending the call, she tossed the phone back into baby Emerald's diaper bag. Picking her up, she fixed the bottom of the pink and blue, plaid, cardigan that graced her tiny frame. Smiling at how cute she looked in her outfit with the matching big, bow headband that was around her head, she placed a kiss onto her fat jaws and handed her over to Fatz.

"Here," She stated snapping him from his thoughts. "I'm about to go to the nurse's station and let them know that we're ready so they can hurry the hell up with our discharge papers." She then told him.

Laying baby Emerald into his arms, she exited the room and headed down the halls towards the nurse's station. Passing the nursery, she smiled looking at all, of the little babies that were inside; they were all so precious. Her smile suddenly faded when something in particular caught her attention. Stopping in her tracks she squinted her eyes peering harder into the window, making sure they weren't playing tricks on her and they weren't.

Sitting in the nursery cradling a baby in her arms was, Zaria. She had her head down, and Fragile could only see half of her face, but she was certain that it was her. She still had the same hairstyle in her head from the night she and Fatz had ran into her and Gwahla at Walmart; which was some black and blonde box braids.

Fragile couldn't see the baby but she wanted to, and it was taking everything in her not to go in and be nosey. Just as she'd made up her mind to go in, Zaria got up from her seat, kissed the baby and placed him back in his cubby. After having a brief word with one of the nurses, she headed for the door. Fragile backed herself in a corner, out of eyesight, and waited for her to come out of the nursery. Just as she did Fragile pretended to not be paying attention, making herself have a head on collision with Zaria; bumping right into her.

"Oh my, I'm so sorry." Fragile stated looking directly into her face; she wanted to make sure Zaria knew it was her.

When they locked eyes, Zaria looked like a deer caught in headlights. Swallowing hard, she stared at her without blinking. Alone in private she'd recited the words she would say to, Fragile if she'd ever got a chance to see her alone, but now that it had come to fruition she was at a lost, for words. Her heart was racing like crazy and her palms were sweaty. She didn't know whether to curse Fragile's ass out and blame her for her life being in shambles or to immediately began begging for her business back.

"Uhm, Zaria, right?" Fragile smiled, acting as if she were trying to remember her name.

"Y..yea." Zaria nodded nervously. "I..I'm sorry, who are you?" She asked pretending she couldn't remember who Fragile was. Since she wanted to play dumb, Fragile decided to fuck with her head a little bit.

"Well we've only crossed paths a couple of times but I'm sure you remember exactly who I am; as I do you." Fragile slightly chuckled. "My name is Fragile; I saw you at Marcus's funeral and another time at Walmart with Gwahla. You know, when your water broke." She finished, putting emphasis on her last statement. Zaria caught the shade. Shifting her demeanor, she decided to throw some back.

"Ooh, okay, yeah; I do remember you." she decided to cut the façade. "You're the home wrecking whore that was screwing my finace `."

Fragile slightly chuckled in disbelief. The bitch had gone from keeping it cute to retarded in the blink of an eye.

"I'll take that title." She told her, sucking her teeth. "As long as you take the skank ass bitch who fucked my baby father's best friend and had a baby by him, title." Fragile stepped closer into her space, seeing just how retarded.

"Girl, fuck you!" Zaria spat. You think you better because he chose you? Newsflash, neither one of us has him now; how you like those apples? I've already confessed my sins, so you can move around trying to hit me with that guilt trip, bullshit! If it wasn't for your home wrecking ass, shit wouldn't even be like this in the first place! Marcus and I were happy, but you just had to come in and fuck shit up! YOU; did this! YOU! So, fuck you, bitch!" Zaria seethed, before turning to storm away.

"Oh, and another thing," She quickly made an about face and began storming back into Fragile's direction. "How does it feel to be prancing around the city with the nigga who killed Marcus? Mhm?" She asked throwing Fragile for a loop.

"What?!" Fragile scoffed, frowning with confusion. "What

are you talking about?"

"Your new boy toy; he was well compensated too. Now try sad ass bitch whose sleeping with my baby father's killer, for a title." Zaria winked before walking away.

Fragile stood there speechless as she watched her prance away as if she'd won. What was the fuck she talking about? Forgetting all about her trip to the nurse's station, she turned around and made her way back to her room. Going in, she made sure to close the door behind her before getting straight to it.

"Did you get paid to kill Emerald's father?" Fragile asked expecting the truth.

Fatz' head sprung up like a Jack in a box and the confused look on his face read that he was caught totally off guard.

"Where that come from?" He asked.

"That doesn't matter, just answer the damn question. Were you paid to kill my child's father or not?!"

"Come on, man; we not about to do this right here, right now." Fatz tried calming her down. "Let's just get baby girl together and we can talk about this on the ride home." He told her, still curious as to how the hell she'd found out. Last time he checked she was going to the nurse's station to get discharge papers; now she was all up in his grill ready to rip his head off.

"Fuck that! Matter fact, give me my fuckin daughter!" Fragile snapped, snatching baby Emerald from his grasp, causing her to cry a bit.

"Aye, watch how the fuck you, handling her!" Fatz seethed. "you need to calm down!"

"Shut up! Don't tell me how to handle my daughter; this is MY daughter!" Fragile shot back. "Now what you need to do is start fuckin talking and tell me what the fuck is up, because I'm about two seconds from calling security to have them escort you the fuck up out of here!" she finished, meaning every word. Pissed was an understatement as to how she felt.

"Aight, fine. Since you wanna talk about it, let's talk about it." Fatz stated frustrated as hell. He had better ways of telling Fragile about the situation but since the shit had somehow already hit the fan, he decided to come clean about it all.

"YES! Yes, I was paid to do it, but this was before I knew you." He confessed, causing Fragile's mouth and heart to drop at her feet.

"Gwahla set up the hit, and we did the job. I never knew that you were his girl until the night we ran into Gwahla and you told me how you knew him; that's when I put all the shit together. I wanted to tell you, I tried to; you told me you didn't want to hear if the shit was bad. Not saying that's a good enough reason but still, you were going through enough. I promise I didn't mean for shit to happen like this, you gotta believe me." Fatz stressed, letting everything out.

Fragile stood as stiff as stone, her eyes piercing a hole through Fatz. Tears began to coat her cheeks as everything he'd said settled into her brain; she was furious. She'd had this nigga in her home, she'd been in his bed, on top of that he'd held her daughter; all the while being the one who killed her father. Fragile felt just as disgusting and dirty as Zaria and Gwahla, if not worse.

"How much did he pay you?" Fragile questioned through gritted teeth.

"Come on, Fragile, really? Does that even matter?"

"HOW MUCH, DID HE FUCKIN PAY YOU?!" She raised her voice just loud enough for him to know she was serious.

"250,000." Fatz sighed.

"Was it worth it?" She asked soaked in her tears.

"To be honest, now that I know you were hurt behind it all, no." He stated sincerely.

"Tuh! You don't know shit about hurt!" Fragile shot, baffled.

How dare him patronize her. "You got 48 hours to put that muthafucka Gwahla out of his misery or I'm going to the police and telling them everything I know. After that I don't ever want to see you or hear from you again. Now, get out." She finished, meaning every word.

"Fragile come on we can ta..."

"GET OUUUT!" she screamed; this time loud enough for anyone to hear.

Fatz threw his hands up in surrender. Taking one last look at her and baby girl, he turned and walked out the door. After hearing the door close, Fragile broke down in tears. Taking a seat in the rocking chair she held baby Emerald tight, as she rocked back and forth. Her heart just couldn't catch a break.

∞∞∞

When ya wrist like this, you don't check the forecast

Everyday it's gon rain

Made a brick through a brick, I ain't whip up shit

This pure cocaine, yeah

From the streets but I got a lil sense, but I
had to go coupe, no brain

I ain't worried bout you, ima do what I do

And I do my thang

Chubbz pulled up in front of Teyanna's apartment complex bumping Lil Baby's hit song *Pure Cocaine*. Placing the car in park, he turned down the radio and looked over at Teyanna, who was staring out of the window looking as if she'd just lost her puppy. Which was odd because when they'd left the hospital, she was the happiest punk in the penitentiary.

"What's wrong, gorgeous?" Chubbz asked, reaching over and

placing his tatted up, hand on top of hers.

Fragile looked from her apartment door to Chubbz, then back at her apartment. Inhaling deeply, she quickly exhaled while shaking her head from side to side.

"When I was back at the hospital, I was excited as hell to be coming home, but now that I'm here I realize I really don't want to be here. It doesn't even feel like home anymore and I really don't want to go in there to him; I don't want to see him." Teyanna admitted, looking straight ahead with tears escaping her eyes.

Her facial expression was blank but Chubbz knew it was because she was terrified. Little did she know, she didn't have to worry about that shit anymore. He had taken care of her bitch ass problem, so she didn't have to worry about him hurting her ever again. He just hoped when he told her about the shit, she wouldn't flip out on his ass. Sighing deeply, he prayed for the best.

"Look, about that." He began rubbing the back of her hand. "trust me when I tell you, you ain't never gotta worry about that nigga hurting you again, aight." He assured her, meaning every word.

"Tuh," Teyanna sarcastically chuckled, wiping tears from her bottom eyelids. "What makes you so sure? What you do, whoop his ass?" She looked over at him with weary eyes. "Well, thanks." She gave a fake smile. "But you could beat that nigga to a pulp and it still ain't gonna keep him from coming back to fuck with me." She finished.

Burying her face into the palm of her hands, she began to softly sob; she didn't know what else to do. For six years that apartment had been her home and she'd worked damn hard to get. She couldn't believe she was allowing one, punk ass nigga to destroy everything she'd built. Grabbing her by the wrists, Chubbz pulled her hands away from her face. Placing two fingers underneath her chin, he lifted her head up and made her look at him.

"Aye, shhh, shhh. It's all good, baby, believe me. The nigga can't come back from the dead to get you, so you ain't got a damn thing to worry about." He smiled.

"Wait, what?" Teyanna asked making sure she'd heard right.

"I told you I would take care of it and I did. He gone; he ain't never coming back!" Chubbz positioned his hand in the form of a handgun and pretended to shoot.

"Are you serious?"

"If I'm lyin I'm flying; and you don't see no wings on my fuckin back, do you? That shit was crazy, you should have seen that nigga; begging for his life like a lil bitch." He chuckled bragging about it. "Speaking of bitches, matter of fact, I got something to show you!" He laughed harder, reaching into his pocket for his phone. Pulling it out he went to his photo gallery.

Teyanna looked at him as if he'd lost his mind; she couldn't believe what she was hearing. Just the thought of him having the nerve to tell her, gave her chills. He acted as if he'd made an accomplishment instead of committing cold blooded murder. It was right then when she knew that the nigga was really, crazy.

Pulling up the photos, Chubbz turned his phone around and showed them to her. Teyanna's mouth hit the floor in shock once noticing Quincy chained up like a bitch with a gag ball stuffed into his mouth. What made her cringe was how oily he was, and the way he had his ass tooted in the air. What type of sick shit were they on?

"You did this to him?" She asked, her hand cupped over her mouth in disbelief.

"Nah, fuck nah! His queer ass was already like that when we found him. Him and some other faggot was up in there drilling each other's assholes; I smoked both they nasty asses." Chubbz told her.

"Good!" Teyanna spat coldly, catching him off guard. Chubbz looked at her sideways.

"Wait, you not mad?" He asked in disbelief.

"Hell, nah!" She scoffed. "That muthafucka beat my ass damn near the whole time we were together, I've been waiting on somebody to put a bullet into his brain. I wish it could've been me." She wiped the excess tears from her eyes. "And to find out he was on the down low puts the icing on the cake; that nigga deserved to die. Playing with people's lives and shit." She grimaced, shaking her head.

"Well damn gangsta!" Chubbz chortled. "here I was scared to tell you I'd murked the nigga, and you don't even give a fuck."

"I'm supposed, to? Hell, if I would have known, I would have asked you to take a picture so I could see the bastard dead for myself!" she sucked her teeth.

"Ah hell nah, you hot!" he laughed. "I can't do no shit like that."

"I know, I know; I'm just saying." Teyanna giggled.

"Plus, we had to get the fuck up out of there and call the cleaning crew so that shit wouldn't come back to you." Chubbz then told her, causing her to stop in mid chuckle.

"Wait, are you telling me ya'll killed him in my apartment?!" Teyanna asked, eyes as big as a doe.

"Uhh, yea; where else was I gonna catch the nigga at?" Chubbz asked shrugging, like the shit wasn't rocket science.

"Fuck, I don't know! But I have to live there!" she fussed.

"Okay, and you still can. You can't even tell it was just brains splattered all over that muthafucka, I promise. I went and checked before I came and got you." He assured her, like telling her brains were once all over her apartment was going to make the shit any better. It only made it worse.

"Oh hell, no! I can't live there anymore. Just the thought of people being killed in there freaks me the fuck out! I don't care if it was Quincy. Hell, to think about it, that's even worse. He might decide to come back and beat my ass in spirit one day!" Teyanna snapped. Oh, noooo; I'm sorry, but you gotta get me a new place or else, I'm moving in with you." She slumped back in her seat folding her arms across her chest, meaning every word.

Chubbz let out a small chuckle, as he shook his head. As much as he wanted to fuck with her, he couldn't help but respect her decision. What woman would want to live in an apartment that she knew her ex was killed in? It didn't matter how she felt about him, it was just the principle. So, he understood.

"Aight, where you you wanna live?" he asked.

"Anywhere but here!" Teyanna cringed, quivering in disgust.

"Well, yo ass better get to looking cause ya ass damn sure ain't moving in with me." He joked.

"Fuck you," she nudged him in the arm with her good, hand.

"When?" he asked serious as heart attack; he hadn't had any ass since he'd met her, so he was ready.

Teyanna chuckle flipping him the bird. As much as she hated to admit it, she was falling for him. Even though he was a natural born asshole, he had a heart of gold, and he showed that he cared for her in more ways than one. She hadn't even given him the booty yet and he was already making boyfriend moves. That's how she knew it was real.

"I'm just playing. You bout wouldn't want to move with me anyway, my feet stink." He told her.

"Oh my gosh! Shut up, Byron." She laughed.

"Aight, I'm just telling you. While you think a nigga playing, ima make you rub these bitches." He told her, cranking the car back up. "I know my bitch love me, cause she rub my feet, aye!" he then recited Blac Youngsta's lyrics. "you gon rub my feet, baby?" he turned to Teyanna.

"Oh, my gawd, I hate you!" she giggled shaking her head.

Pulling off from in front of Teyanna's apartment complex,

he turned his radio up. Until they found her a place of her own, he figured she could crash at his pad. Even though he had a few places she could stay alone, he wanted to take her back the home he laid his head at every night; she was too special to him to be left alone. He just hoped agreeing to getting her a new place kept her mind off, of the shit he had to tell her next.

Chapter Nine

"Glammy, can I watch TV until I fall asleep? I don't wanna be in the dark, it's scary." MJ told Ms. Jefferson as she tucked him in for bed.

It was a little after 10pm on a Sunday and he was way up past his bedtime, but she only had herself to blame for that. They were having so much fun playing board games and watching movies, she'd lost track of time.

"Sure, what would you like to watch, my dear?" She asked, pulling the covers over his little body.

"Paw Patrol!"

"Paw Patrol?" She asked just excited as he was. MJ began nodding his head yes, with a big warm smile gracing his precious face. "Well, let's see what Glammy can do about that!"

Reaching over onto the nightstand, Ms. Jefferson grabbed the remote. Hitting the power button, she turned the television on and went straight to the guide. Flipping through it, she looked for Paw Patrol on all, of the children networks. After not getting any luck, she turned to MJ.

"Well son, Paw Patrol isn't on right now." She told him.

"Uh huh, it's always on. You gota go On Demand, Glammy."

Ms. Jefferson slightly chuckled. "Aren't you the little genius. What you know about On Demand?" She asked.

"I don't know." He shrugged. "I just know mommy says Paw Patrol is there."

"Okay, well I'll take you and your mommy's word for it."

Ms. Jefferson continued to laugh as she went On Demand and began searching. MJ was just too smart for his own four, year old good. Just as he'd said, Paw Patrol was On Demanded. Pulling up the show he'd requested, she hit the *SELECT* button then play. Once the show came on, MJ immediately began singing the theme song. Placing the remote back down on the nightstand, Ms. Jefferson turned out the light.

"Thank you, Glammy!"

"You're so very welcome!" She leaned over and kissed his forehead. "Now, Glammy is going to the kitchen so I can put dinner up, okay."

"Okay." MJ replied sweetly, his eyes glued to the television.

Getting up from the edge of the bed, Ms. Jefferson made her exit and headed for the lower level of her home. She made sure to leave MJ's bedroom door open so that the light from the hallway could shine through and he wouldn't be afraid. Once making it down the stairs and in the kitchen, she proceeded to put her Sunday dinner away; which consisted of beef pot roast smothered in onions and gray, cabbage, sweet potatoes, corn bread and banana pudding.

Every Sunday, Ms. Jefferson made it her business to cook a big meal. It was times like that when she missed her son the most. He loved his mother's cooking and there wasn't a Sunday that went by where he wasn't there with his plate full. Especially during football season.

Ms. Jefferson smiled as she thought about the good ole days. A tear began to escape her eye as she stood at the kitchen sink, washing the dishes. Never in a million years did she think she would have to bury her son; her baby boy at that. Children were supposed to bury their parents, not the other way around. It just wasn't fair.

Ding, Dong!

Breaking her from her thoughts, Ms. Jefferson heard the

doorbell. Looking over at the clock on the stove, she noticed it was 10:45 and immediately began to wonder who could be ringing her bell at that time of night. Grabbing the dry, dish towel she dried her hands and tears, before tossing it onto the table and heading for the front door. When she made it, she looked out of the peephole. Recognizing who it was, she let out a heavy breath and began unlocking the door. Swinging it open, she stared at Gwahla through the glass of her screen door. Giving him a smug look, she unlocked it as well, pushing it open.

"Heeeey, ma, what's up?!" A clearly drunken Gwahla, brushed pass her, staggering into her home. Not only could she tell that he had been drinking, but she could smell it in the wind as he walked in.

"Terrence." Ms. Jefferson replied disgusted in more ways than one. "What are you doing here?" She then asked closing the door, behind him.

"Well you said you wanted me to start back visiting more, so here I am!" Gwahla held out his arms like he was a damn grand prize or some shit. "What you cook today? I know you threw down, it's Sunday." He then headed for the kitchen, just knowing she'd prepared a meal.

Ms. Jefferson followed behind as she watched him head straight for the refrigerator. Opening it up, Gwahla got excited as he noticed the Tupperware stacked neatly on the top shelf, filled with leftovers. Just as he were about to reach his hand inside to get the containers, she swiftly kicked the refrigerator door closed; centimeters away from taking his arm off. Giving him the look, he immediately realized what he'd done wrong. Making his way to the double-sided sink, he commenced to washing his hands.

Ms. Jefferson took a seat at the island and remained silent. Staring at Gwahla's back in rage, she began to think of how much hate she'd developed for the man she once called her son. A man that she had taken in, fed, clothed, and placed in the best schools after he'd lost his mother. A man that crawled into her bed as a little boy for her to hold him, to keep the nightmare monsters away at night; was the very same man that betrayed her family like she hadn't done a damn thing for him and hurt her to the core.

"I remember when you and your mother first joined the church, you were so shy; just the cutest little thing." Ms. Jefferson slightly smiled, as an image of Terrance as a child flashed through her mind. "You and Marcus clicked instantly; you were like the little brother he'd always wanted. You two would split everything! I never understood that when you both could just have your own, but Marcus would always say *noooo, me and my brother gotta share.*" Ms. Jefferson chuckled as she imitated her son's voice as a kid.

"When your mother died, it got worse because he felt as if he had to protect you from everything. It hurt him so bad to see you hurt; when you would cry, he would come to me crying because you were crying. He loved you; blood didn't make a difference; you were his brother."

Gwahla paused as he stared at the wall in front of him. Though Ms. Jefferson wasn't his biological mother, he knew her well enough to know when something was bothering her. Any time she made a trip down memory lane, reminiscing on the good times, there was something on her heart.

"You were like two peas in a pot. I remember he bought you your first car, got you your first house, hell he even gave you your first job." She slightly chuckled. "My boy was such a good brother to you."

Having enough of her guilt game, Gwahla slammed the utensils he was using to make his plate, down onto the counter. Turning to face Ms. Jefferson, he looked at her with fire in his eyes.

"And, what is all that supposed to mean? I was just as good to that nigga as he was to me!" he shouted, causing Ms. Jefferson to slightly flinch. "You sound like him with all that bullshit; throwing up what he's done for a nigga. I worked for that! Anything that nigga had ever done for me, I worked for that shit! Never forget that! I was entitled to that plus more; so, miss me with that he was good to me shit!" He finished sucking his teeth.

Ms. Jefferson sat as stiff as stone, flabbergasted by the words that were leaving Gwahla's lips. It was as if the man standing before her was a complete, stranger. They say a drunk tongue speaks a sober mind and heart but never in a million years did she expect to hear him speak such things. The venom in his tone and the blackness in his eyes showed her that he held a lot of hatred in his heart for her son. It was her first time witnessing it, but she could tell that it was real; she felt it.

"So, is that why you felt you were entitled to his woman?" Ms. Jefferson asked, revealing she knew all about their dirty secret. Gwahla smacked his lips and waved her off.

"Please, he didn't love her. I'm a way better man to her than he could've ever been. He took her for granted just like he takes everything for granted. Treat you like a scum of the earth then pacify you with his money. Marcus was a bitch; and I blame you because you couldn't keep your titty out of his mouth when we were growing u.."

SLAP!

Gwahla tried finishing his statement but before he could, Ms. Jefferson had reached over the island, and smacked spit from his lips.

"I think it's time for you to leave, cause what you WON'T do, is sit up in my face, in my house and disrespect I nor my son! Now I ain't no killer, but I damn sure know some, so if I find out you or that skank ass whore of yours had something to do with my son's murder, you won't have to worry about the police getting you because they won't be able to find you; I'll be somewhere feeding your black ass to the fishes. And that's a PROMISE! Now get the fuck out of my house!" She seethed with venom. If looks could kill, he would have been dead right then and there.

Not saying a word, Gwahla gave Ms. Jefferson one last evil glare before turning to storm out of the kitchen. Before leaving out, he made sure to knock all, of her leftovers off, of the kitchen counter and onto the floor, slamming the front door behind him.

∞∞∞

"Man, what the fuck is this nigga on, making all these fuckin stops and shit! We been following his ass for over a fuckin hour; I'm fuckin hungry!" Chubbz barked as they sat outside of Ms. Jefferson's crib, waiting on Gwahla to come out.

He and Fatz had been trailing him since he'd left Tom's, a local bar located in the Central Westend area, and he'd made several stops during their journey. Getting his location from one of their young homies, they'd put their plan in action to erase the nigga for good.

"All I know is wherever he stops at next, I'm just gon hop out and gun his ass down. I'm tired of trailing this nigga." Fatz replied with murder in his eyes.

It hadn't even been 24 hours since Fragile called the hit and he was already on Gwahla's ass. Though he felt in his heart that she wouldn't give him up, Fatz still wanted the nigga dead. Mainly because he knew that he was the one talking to them people. Another reason being, he was a bitch and he just didn't like his snake ass.

"Shit, I'm down! I been ready to hop out and get the nigga, I just know you want to be the one to pull the trigger. I know you tryna get ya bitch back and shit, so I ain't gon step on ya toes." Chubbz winked, like he was really looking out. Fatz grimaced at his little brother as he sucked his teeth.

"Fuck you, aight. Don't start with yo weak ass jokes just because Teyanna was all good about you smokin Quincy's bitch ass!" He shot.

140

"Aye man, chill," Chubbz chortled throwing his hands up in surrender. "I ain't even tryna be funny, I'm just saying."

"Yea, whatever. Just shut up and get ready, the nigga coming out." Fatz told him as he watched Gwahla come storming out of Ms. Jefferson's crib.

They watched as he hopped into his ride, quickly starting it up and skirting off. Fatz started his engine and pulled of behind him, being sure not to get to close. They followed him for about another 15 minutes before he pulled up to a fat ass crib, located in the Ladue area. Parking a few houses down, Fatz killed the engine and hit his lights.

"Aight, you stay put, ima go in, handle that and I'll be right back out." He then told Chubbz, pulling out a chrome, snub nose, 38.

"Ah hell nah! You think I'm finna sit out here and wait while you go in there and have all the fun? I at least wanna watch." Chubbz snapped as if he were about to go in there and make a porno instead of killing a nigga.

"Nigga, do you see where we at?! Ain't nobody got time for yo shit tonight, I am not going to jail out here in this white ass neighborhood fuckin with you. Just stay put and I'll be back before you know it." Fatz shot back, sliding out of the whip before her could reply. Chubbz punched the dashboard once the driver's door closed.

"Ole bitch! He always gotta be the one to have all the fun." He seethed, seriously upset.

Once out of the car Fatz crept slowly towards the house of the driveway he saw Gwahla pull into. He watched as he exited his car and stumbled towards the door. As he was fiddling with his keys, he failed to hear Fatz walk up behind him. It wasn't until he felt the coldness of steel pressed to the back of his medulla, before he realized he had company, causing him to sober up a lot fater than he wanted to.

"Don't freeze now, nigga. Continue to open that muthafuckin door and you bet not look back!" Fatz demanded, pressing the gun harder into his scalp.

"You picked the wrong nigga to rob, homie. You must don't know who the fuck I am." Gwahla chuckled unlocking the door and opening it.

"Shut yo bitch ass up! You ain't no fuckin body." Fatz barked. "Now get the fuck in the house!" He forcefully pushed him into his crib, almost making him hit the floor face first. Closing the door behind them, he kept his gun aimed at Gwahla.

"Damn nigga, this fat! This all you? You eating good since you had ya boy killed, huh? Not bad." Fatz nodded his head in approval as he looked around. He had to admit, the bitch was nice as fuck and he had it laid out.

"How the fuck you find out where I live."

"Ah man, is that how you talk to all your first, time guest?" Fatz asked sarcastically. "No wonder nobody likes yo ass."

"What the fuck do you want from me, you've ran through a quarter mil that fast? Well, guess what? I ain't got shit else for you, so you can get the fuck up out of my house."

"Oooooh, a lil bit more money made you grow a lil more balls too I see." Fatz chuckled. "Nigga I'll blow yo muthafuckin snitch ass brains out!" He then grimaced, biting into his bottom lip.

Gwahla chuckled hysterically.

"Oooh, that's why you're here. Police came snooping round to shit so you think a nigga a snitch. Newsflash, I'm a street nigga. Never been a rat and I don't fuck wit em." He lied, slowly reaching for the gun he had tucked in the back of his pants. "Now as I asked you before, get the fuck out before I have to use my first amendment right." He finished, securing his hand around the butt of his gun.

"Nigga who you think you fooling? You been pussy and you always gon be pussy. You ain't killing shit or letting shit die; you think I'm worried about yo punk ass threats?" Fatz was so busy taunting him, he failed to see him draw down.

"See, that's where your wrong, you ain't the only killer!"

POW! POW! POW! POW!

Before Fatz knew it, shots rang out in his direction.

To be continued....

WANT TO INTERACT WITH T'ANN MARIE & HER TEAM? JOIN OUR READERS GROUP ON FACEBOOK @ T'ANN MARIE PRESENTS: THE HOUSE OF URBAN LITERACY! WIN PRIZES, BE APART OF LIVE BOOK DISCUSSIONS & MORE!

T'Ann Marie
PRESENTS

Are you looking for a publishing home that will mold you to become a better writer?

T'Ann Marie Presents, is now accepting submissions in the following genres:

*Urban Fiction
*Romance
*Street Lit
*Paranormal
*BWWM
*Erotica
*Women's Fiction
*Christian Fiction

For consideration, please submit the first 3 chapters of your finished manuscript & contact information to:

TAnnMarieSubs@gmail.com

Let us make your dreams, Reality!

Want to join our mailing list?!

Just send your email address by text to:

Text

TMPUPNEXT

to 22828 to get started.

Message and data rates may apply.

Made in the USA
Monee, IL
14 December 2019